Richard Ford

WILDLIFE

BLOOMSBURY

I wish to thank my friends Carl Navarre and Gary
Taylor for their special generosities, which helped
me write this book.
R.F.

First published in Great Britain by Collins Harvill 1990
This paperback edition published 2006

Bloomsbury Publishing Plc, 36 Soho Square, London W1D 3QY

A CIP catalogue record for this book
is available from the British Library

ISBN 0 7475 8523 7
9780747585237

10 9 8 7 6 5 4 3 2 1

Printed in Great Britain by Clays Ltd, St Ives plc

www.bloomsbury.com/richardford

Kristina

IN THE FALL OF 1960, when I was sixteen and my father was for a time not working, my mother met a man named Warren Miller and fell in love with him. This was in Great Falls, Montana, at the time of the Gypsy Basin oil boom, and my father had brought us there in the spring of that year from Lewiston, Idaho, in the belief that people – small people like him – were making money in Montana or soon would be, and he wanted a piece of that good luck before all of it collapsed and was gone in the wind.

My father was a golfer. A teaching pro. He had been to college though not to the war. And since 1944, the year when I was born and two years after he married my mother, he had worked at that – at golf – at the small country clubs and public courses in the towns near where he'd grown up, around Colfax and the Palouse Hills of eastern Washington

7

State. And during that time, the years when *I* was growing up, we had lived in Coeur d'Alene and McCall, Idaho, and in Endicott and Pasco and Walla Walla, where both he and my mother had gone to college and where they had met and gotten married.

My father was a natural athlete. His own father had owned a clothing store in Colfax and made a good living, and he had learned to play golf on the kinds of courses he taught on. He could play every sport—basketball and ice hockey and throw horse shoes, and he had played baseball in college. But he loved the game of golf because it was a game other people found difficult and that was easy for him. He was a smiling, handsome man with dark hair—not tall but with delicate hands and a short fluid swing that was wonderful to see but never strong enough to move him into the higher competition of the game. He was good at teaching people to play golf, though. He knew how to discuss the game patiently, in ways to make you think you had a talent for it, and people liked being around him. Sometimes he and my mother would play together and I would go along with them and pull their cart, and I knew he knew how they looked—good-looking, young, happy. My father was soft-spoken and good-natured and optimistic—not slick in the way someone might think. And though it is not a usual life to be a golfer, to make your living at it the way anyone does who is a salesman or a doctor, my father was in a sense not a usual kind of man: he was innocent and he was honest, and it is possible he was suited perfectly for the life he had made.

In Great Falls my father took a job two days a week at the air base, at the course there, and worked the rest of the time at the club for-members-only, across the river. The Wheatland Club that was called. He worked extra because, he said, in good times people wanted to learn a game like golf, and good times rarely lasted long enough. He was thirty-nine then, and I think he hoped he'd meet someone there, someone who'd give him a tip, or let him in on a good deal

8

in the oil boom, or offer him a better job, a chance that would lead him and my mother and me to something better.

We rented a house on Eighth Street North in an older neighborhood of single-story, brick-and-frame houses. Ours was yellow and had a low, paled fence across the front of it and a weeping birch tree in the side yard. Those streets are not far from the train tracks and are across the river from the refinery where a bright flame burned at all hours from the stack above the metal tank buildings. I could hear the shift whistles blow in the morning when I woke up, and late at night the loud whooshing of machinery processing crude oil from the wildcat fields north of us.

My mother did not have a job in Great Falls. She had worked as a bookkeeper for a dairy company in Lewiston, and in the other towns where we had lived she had been a substitute teacher in math and science – the subjects she enjoyed. She was a pretty, small woman who had a good sense for a joke and who could make you laugh. She was two years younger than my father, and had met him in college in 1941 and liked him, and simply left with him when he'd taken a job in Spokane. I don't know what she thought my father's reasons were for leaving his job in Lewiston and coming to Great Falls. Maybe she noticed something about him – that it was an odd time in his life when his future had begun to seem different to him, as if he couldn't rely on it just to take care of itself as it had up until then. Or maybe there were other reasons, and because she loved him she went along with him. But I do not think she ever wanted to come to Montana. She liked eastern Washington, liked the better weather there, where she had been a girl. She thought it would be too cold and lonely in Great Falls, and people would not be easy to meet. Yet she must've believed at the time that this was a normal life she was living, moving, and working when she could, having a husband and a son, and that it was fine.

*　　*　　*

The summer of that year was a time of forest fires. Great Falls is where the plains begin, but south and west and east of there are mountains. You could see mountains on clear days from the streets of town—sixty miles away the high eastern front of the Rocky Mountains themselves, blue and clear-cut, running to Canada. In early July, fires started in the timber canyons beyond Augusta and Choteau, towns that were insignificant to me but that were endangered. Fires began by mysterious causes. They burned on and on through July and August and into September when it was thought that an early fall would bring rains and possibly snow, though that is not what happened.

Spring had been a dry season and lasted dry into summer. I was a city boy and knew nothing about crops or timber, but we all heard that farmers believed dryness forecasted dryness, and read in the paper that standing timber was drier than wood put in a kiln, and that if farmers were smart they would cut their wheat early to save losses. Even the Missouri River dropped to a low stage, and fish died, and dry mud flats opened between the banks and the slow stream, and no one boated there.

My father taught golf every day to groups of airmen and their girlfriends, and at the Wheatland Club he played foursomes with ranchers and oilmen and bankers and their wives, whose games he was paid to improve upon and tried to. In the evenings through that summer he would sit at the kitchen table after work, listening to a ball game from the East and drinking a beer, and read the paper while my mother fixed dinner and I did schoolwork in the living room. He would talk about people at the club. 'They're all good enough fellows,' he said to my mother. 'We won't get rich working for rich men, but we might get lucky hanging around them.' He laughed about that. He liked Great Falls. He thought it was wide open and undiscovered, and no one had time to hold you back, and that it was a good time to live there. I don't know what his ideas for himself were then, but he was a man, more than most, who liked to be happy. And it must've seemed as though, just for that time, he had finally come to his right place.

By the first of August the timber fires to the west of us had not been put out, and a haze was in the air so that you could sometimes not see the mountains or where the land met the sky. It was a haze you wouldn't detect if you were inside of it, only if you were on a mountain or in an airplane and could see Great Falls from above. At night, when I stood at the window and looked west up the valley of the Sun River toward the mountains that were blazing, I would taste smoke and smell it, and believe that I saw flames and hills on fire and men moving, though I couldn't see that, could only see a brightening, wide and red and deep above the darkness between the fire and all of us. Twice I even dreamed our house had caught fire, a spark traveling miles on a wind and catching in our roof, consuming everything. Though I knew even in this dream that the world would spin on and we would survive, and the fire did not matter so much. I did not understand, of course, what it meant not to survive.

Such a fire could not help changing things, and there was a feeling in Great Falls, some attitude in general, that was like discouragement. There were stories in the paper, wild stories. Indians were said to have set fires to get the jobs putting them out. A man was seen driving a loggers' road throwing flaming sticks out his truck window. Poachers were to blame. A peak far back in the Marshall Mountains was said to have been struck by lightning a hundred times in an hour. My father heard on the golf course that criminals were fighting the fire, murderers and rapists from Deer Lodge, men who'd volunteered but then slipped away and back to civilized life.

No one, I think, thought Great Falls would burn. Too many miles separated us from the fire, too many other towns would have to go first – too much bad luck falling one way. But people wet the roofs of their houses, and no one was allowed to burn ditches. Planes took off every day carrying men to jump into the flames, and west of us smoke rose like thunderheads, as if the fire itself could make rain. When the wind stiffened in the afternoons, we all knew that the fire had jumped a trench line or rushed forward or exploded into some untouched place, and that we were all affected, even if we never saw flames or felt the heat.

I was then beginning the eleventh grade in Great Falls High School and was trying to play football, a game I did not like and wasn't good at, and tried to play only because my father thought I could make friends by playing. There were days, though, that we sat out football practice because the doctor said smoke would scar our lungs and we wouldn't feel it. I would go on those days and meet my father at the Wheatland Club – the base course having closed because of the fire danger – and hit practice balls with him late in the day. My father began to work fewer days as the summer went on, and was home more. People did not come to the club because of the smoke and the dryness. He taught fewer lessons, saw fewer of the members he had met and made friends with the spring before. He worked more in the pro shop, sold golf equipment and clothes and magazines, rented carts, spent more time collecting balls along the edge of the river by the willows where the driving range ended.

On an afternoon in late September, two weeks after I had started school and the fires in the mountains west of us seemed to be lasting forever, I went with my father out on the driving range with wire baskets. One man was hitting balls off the practice tee far away and to the left of us. I could hear the thwock of the club, then the hiss as the balls arched out into the twilight and bounced toward us. At home, the night before, he and my mother had talked about the election that was coming. They were Democrats. Both their families had been. But my father said on that night that he was considering the Republicans now. Nixon, he said, was a good lawyer. He was not a personable man, but he would stand up to the labor unions.

My mother laughed at him and put her hands over her eyes as if she didn't want to see him. 'Oh, not you, too, Jerry,' she said. 'Are you becoming a right-to-work advocate?' She was joking. I don't think she cared who he voted for, and they did not talk about politics. We were in the kitchen and food was already set out on the table.

'Things feel like they've gone too far in one direction,' my father said. He put his hands on either side of his plate. I heard him breathe. He still had on his golf clothes, green pants and a yellow nylon shirt with a red club emblem on it. There had been a railroad strike during that summer, but he had not talked about unions, and I didn't think it had affected us.

My mother was standing and drying her hands at the sink. 'You're a working man, I'm not,' she said. 'I'll just remind you of that, though.'

'I wish we had a Roosevelt to vote for,' my father said. 'He had a feel for the country.'

'That was just a different time then,' my mother said, and sat down across the metal table from him. She was wearing a blue and white checked dress and an apron. 'Everyone was afraid then, including us. Everything's better now. You forget that.'

'I haven't forgotten anything,' my father said. 'But I'm interested in thinking about the future now.'

'Well,' she said. She smiled at him. 'That's good. I'm glad to hear that. I'm sure Joe's glad of it, too.' And then we ate dinner.

The next afternoon, though, at the end of the driving range by the willows and the river, my father was in a different mood. He had not given a lesson that week, but wasn't tense, and he didn't seem mad at anything. He was smoking a cigarette, something he didn't ordinarily do.

'It's a shame not to work in warm weather,' he said and smiled. He took one of the golf balls out of his basket, drew back and threw it through the willow branches toward the river where it hit down in the mud without a sound. 'How's your football going,' he asked me. 'Are you going to be the next Bob Waterfield?'

'No,' I said. 'I don't think so.'

'I won't be the next Walter Hagen, either,' he said. He liked Walter Hagen. He had a picture of him wearing a broad-brimmed hat and a heavy overcoat, laughing at the camera as he teed off someplace where there was snow on the ground. My father kept that picture inside the closet door in his and my mother's bedroom.

He stood and watched the lone golfer who was driving balls out onto the fairway. We could see him silhouetted. 'There's a man who hits the ball nicely,' he said, watching the man take his club back smoothly, then sweep through his swing. 'He doesn't take chances. Get the ball in the middle of the fairway, then take the margin of error. Let the other guy foul up. That's what Walter Hagen did. The game came naturally to him.'

'Isn't it the same with you,' I asked, because that's what my mother had said, that my father had never needed to practice.

'Yes it is,' my father said, smoking. 'I thought it was easy. There's probably something wrong with that.'

'I don't like football,' I said.

My father glanced at me and then stared at the west where the fire was darkening the sun, turning it purple. 'I liked it,' he said in a dreamy way. 'When I had the ball and ran up the field and dodged people, I liked that.'

'I don't dodge enough,' I said. I wanted to tell this to him because I wanted him to tell me to quit football and do something else. I liked golf and would've been happy to play it.

'I wasn't going to not play golf, though,' he said, 'even

though I'm probably not cagey enough for it.' He was not listening to me, now, though I didn't hold it against him.

Far away at the practice tee I heard a thwock as the lone man drove a ball up into the evening air. There was a silence as my father and I waited for the ball to hit and bounce. But the ball actually hit my father, hit him on the shoulder above the bottom of his sleeve – not hard or even hard enough to cause pain.

My father said, 'Well. For Christ's sake. Look at that.' He looked down at the ball beside him on the ground, then rubbed his arm. We could see the man who'd hit the ball walking back toward the clubhouse, his driver swinging beside him like a walking cane. He had no idea where the balls were falling. He hadn't dreamed he'd hit my father.

My father stood and watched the man disappear into the long white clubhouse building. He stood for a while as if he was listening and could hear something I couldn't hear – laughing possibly, or music from far away. He had always been a happy man, and I think he may simply have been waiting for something to make him feel that way again.

'If you don't like football,' – and he suddenly looked at me as if he'd forgotten I was there – 'then just forget about it. Take up the javelin throw instead. There's a feeling of achievement in that. I did it once.'

'All right,' I said. And I thought about the javelin throw – about how much a javelin would weigh and what it was made of and how hard it would be to throw the right way.

My father was staring toward where the sky was beautiful and dark and full of colors. 'It's on fire out there, isn't it? I can smell it.'

'I can too,' I said, watching.

'You have a clear mind, Joe.' He looked at me. 'Nothing bad will happen to you.'

'I hope not,' I said.

'That's good,' he said, 'I hope so, too.' And we went on

15

then picking up golf balls and walking back toward the clubhouse.

When we had walked back to the pro shop, lights were on inside, and through the glass windows I could see a man sitting alone in a folding chair, smoking a cigar. He had on a business suit, though he had the jacket over his arm and was wearing brown and white golf shoes.

When my father and I stepped inside carrying our baskets of range balls, the man stood up. I could smell the cigar and the clean smell of new golf equipment.

'Hello there, Jerry,' the man said, and smiled and stuck out his hand to my father. 'How'd my form look to you out there?'

'I didn't realize that was you,' my father said, and smiled. He shook the man's hand. 'You have a blueprint swing. You can brag about that.'

'I spray 'em around a bit,' the man said, and put his cigar in his mouth.

'That's everybody's misery,' my father said, and brought me to his side. 'This is my son, Joe, Clarence. This is Clarence Snow, Joe. He's the president of this club. He's the best golfer out here.' I shook hands with Clarence Snow, who was in his fifties and had long fingers, bony and strong, like my father's. He did not shake my hand very hard.

'Did you leave any balls out there, Jerry?' Clarence Snow said, running his hand back through his thin, dark hair and casting a look at the dark course.

'Quite a few,' my father said. 'We lost our light.'

'Do you play this game, too, son?' Clarence Snow smiled at me.

'He's good,' my father said before I could answer anything. He sat down on the other folding chair that had his street shoes under it, and began unlacing his white golf

16

shoes. My father was wearing yellow socks that showed his pale, hairless ankles, and he was staring at Clarence Snow while he loosened his laces.

'I need to have a talk with you, Jerry,' Clarence Snow said. He glanced at me and sniffed his nose.

'That's fine,' my father said. 'Can it wait till tomorrow?'

'No it can't,' Clarence Snow said. 'Would you come up to the office?'

'I certainly will,' my father said. He had his golf shoes off and he raised one foot and rubbed it, then squeezed his toes down. 'The tools of ignorance,' he said, and smiled at me.

'This won't take much time,' Clarence Snow said. Then he walked out the front door, leaving my father and me alone in the lighted shop.

My father sat back in his folding chair, stretched his legs in front of him, and wiggled his toes in his yellow socks. 'He'll fire me,' he said. 'That's what this'll be.'

'Why do you think that?' I said. And it shocked me.

'You don't know about these things, son,' my father said. 'I've been fired before. These things have a feel to them.'

'Why would he do that?' I said.

'Maybe he thinks I fucked his wife,' my father said. I hadn't heard him say that kind of thing before, and it shocked me, too. He was staring out the window into the dark. 'Of course, I don't know if he has a wife.' My father began putting on his street shoes, which were black loafers, shiny and new and thick-soled. 'Maybe I won some money from one of his friends. He doesn't have to have a reason.' He slid the white shoes under the chair and stood up. 'Wait in here,' he said. And I knew he was mad, but did not want me to know he was. He liked to make you believe everything was fine and for everybody to be happy if they could be. 'Is that okay?' he said.

'It's okay,' I said.

'Think about some pretty girls while I'm gone,' he said, and smiled at me.

17

Then he walked, almost strolling, out of the little pro shop and up toward the clubhouse, leaving me by myself with the racks of silver golf clubs and new leather bags and shoes and boxes of balls—all the other tools of my father's trade, still and silent around me like treasures.

When my father came back in twenty minutes he was walking faster than when he'd left. He had a piece of yellow paper stuck up in his shirt pocket, and his face looked tight. I was sitting on the chair Clarence Snow had sat on. My father picked up his white shoes off the green carpet, put them under his arm, then walked to the cash register and began taking money out of the trays.

'We should go,' he said in a soft voice. He was putting money in his pants pocket.

'Did he fire you,' I asked.

'Yes he did.' He stood still for a moment behind the open cash register as if the words sounded strange to him, or had other meanings. He looked like a boy my own age doing something he shouldn't be doing and trying to do it casually. Though I thought maybe Clarence Snow had told him to clean out the cash register before he left and all that money was his to keep. 'Too much of a good living, I guess,' he said. Then he said, 'Look around here, Joe. See if you see anything you want.' He looked around at the clubs and the leather golf bags and shoes, the sweaters and clothes in glass cases. All things that cost a lot of money, things my father liked. 'Just take it,' he said. 'It's yours.'

'I don't want anything,' I said.

My father looked at me from behind the cash register. 'You don't want anything? All this expensive stuff?'

'No,' I said.

'You've got good character, that's your problem. Not that it's much of a problem.' He closed the cash register drawer. 'Bad luck's got a sour taste, doesn't it?'

'Yes sir,' I said.

'Do you want to know what he said to me?' My father leaned on the glass countertop with his palms down. He smiled at me, as if he thought it was funny.

'What?' I said.

'He said he didn't require an answer from me, but he thought I was stealing things. Some yokel lost a wallet out on the course, and they couldn't figure anybody else who could do it. So I was elected.' He shook his head. 'I'm not a stealer. Do you know it? That's not me.'

'I know it,' I said. And I didn't think he was. I thought I was more likely to be a stealer than he was, and I wasn't one either.

'I was too well liked out here, that's my problem,' he said. 'If you help people they don't like you for it. They're like Mormons.'

'I guess so,' I said.

'When you get older,' my father said. And then he seemed to stop what he was about to say. 'If you want to know the truth don't listen to what people tell you,' was all he said.

He walked around the cash register, holding his white shoes, his pants pockets full of money. 'Let's go now,' he said. He turned off the light when he got to the door, held it open for me, and we walked out into the warm summer night.

When we'd driven back across the river into Great Falls and up Central, my father stopped at the grocery a block from our house, went in and bought a can of beer and came back and sat in the car seat with the door open. It had become cooler with the sun gone and felt like a fall night, although it was dry and the sky was light blue and full of stars. I could smell beer on my father's breath and knew he was thinking about the conversation he would have with my mother when we got home, and what that would be like.

'Do you know what happens,' he said, 'when the very thing you wanted least to happen happens to you?' We were sitting in the glow of the little grocery store. Traffic was moving behind us along Central Avenue, people going home from work, people with things they liked to do on their minds, things they looked forward to.

'No,' I said. I was thinking about throwing the javelin at that moment, a high arching throw into clear air, coming down like an arrow, and of my father throwing it when he was my age.

'Nothing at all does,' he said, and he was quiet for several seconds. He raised his knees and held his beer can with both hands. 'We should probably go on a crime spree. Rob this store or something. Bring everything down on top of us.'

'I don't want to do that,' I said.

'I'm probably a fool,' my father said, and shook his beer can until the beer fizzed softly inside. 'It's just hard to see my opportunities right this minute.' He didn't say anything else for a while. 'Do you love your dad?' he said in a normal voice, after some time had passed.

'Yes,' I said.

'Do you think I'll take good care of you?'

'Yes,' I said. 'I think so.'

'I will,' he said.

My father shut the car door and sat a moment looking out the windshield at the grocery, where people were inside moving back and forth behind the plate-glass windows. 'Choices don't always feel exactly like choices,' he said. He started the car then, and he put his hand on my hand just like you would on a girl's. 'Don't be worried about things,' he said. 'I feel calm now.'

'I'm not worried,' I said. And I wasn't, because I thought things would be fine. And even though I was wrong, it is still not so bad a way to set your mind toward the unknown just when you are coming into the face of it.

AFTER THAT NIGHT IN early September things began to move more quickly in our life and to change. Our life at home changed. The life my mother and father lived changed. The world, for as little as I'd thought about it or planned on it, changed. When you are sixteen you do not know what your parents know, or much of what they understand, and less of what's in their hearts. This can save you from becoming an adult too early, save your life from becoming only theirs lived over again—which is a loss. But to shield yourself—as I didn't do —seems to be an even greater error, since what's lost is the truth of your parents' life and what you should think about it, and beyond that, how you should estimate the world you are about to live in.

On the night my father came home from losing his job at the Wheatland Club, he told my mother about it straight out and they both acted as if it was a kind of joke. My mother did not get mad or seem upset or ask him why he had gotten fired. They both laughed about it. When we ate supper my mother sat at the table and seemed to be thinking. She said she could not get a job substituting until the term ended, but she would go to the school board and put her name in. She said other people would come to my father for work when it was known he was free, and that this was an opportunity in disguise – the reason we had come here – and that Montanans did not know gold when they saw it. She smiled at him when she said that. She said I could get a job, and I said I would. She said maybe she should become a banker, though she would need to finish college for that. And she laughed. Finally she said, 'You can do other things, Jerry. Maybe you've played enough golf for this lifetime.'

After dinner, my father went into the living room and listened to the news from a station we could get from Salt Lake after dark, and went to sleep on the couch still wearing his golf clothes. Late in the night they went into their room and closed the door. I heard their voices, talking. I heard my mother laugh again. And then my father laughed and said, loudly, still laughing, 'Don't threaten me. I can't be threatened.' And later on my mother said, 'You've just had your feelings hurt, Jerry, is all.' After a while I heard the bathtub running with water, and I knew my father was sitting in the bathroom talking to my mother while she took her bath, which was a thing he liked doing. And later I heard their door close and their light click off and the house become locked in silence.

And then for a time after that my father did not seem to take an interest in working. In a few days the Wheatland Club called – a man who was not Clarence Snow said someone had made a mistake. I talked to the man, who gave me the message to give to my father, but my father did not call back. The air base called him, but again he did not accept. I know he did not sleep well. I could hear doors close at night and glasses tapping together. Some mornings I would look out my bedroom window and he would be in the backyard in the chill air practicing with a driver, hitting a plastic ball from one property line to the next, walking in his long easy gait as if nothing was bothering him. Other days he would take me on long drives after school, to Highwood and to Belt and Geraldine, which are the towns east of Great Falls, and let me drive the car on the wheat prairie roads where I could be no danger to anyone. And once we drove across the river to Fort Benton and sat in the car and watched golfers playing on the tiny course there above the town.

Eventually, my father began to leave the house in the morning like a man going to a job. And although we did not know where he went, my mother said she thought he went downtown, and that he had left jobs before and that it was always scary for a while, but that finally he would stand up to things and go back and be happy. My father began to wear different kinds of clothes, khaki pants and flannel shirts, regular clothes I saw people wearing, and he did not talk about golf any more. He talked some about the fires, which still burned late in September in the canyons above Allen Creek and Castle Reef—names I knew about from the *Tribune*. He talked in a more clipped way then. He told me the smoke from such fires went around the world in five days and that the amount of timber lost there would've built fifty thousand homes the size of ours. One Friday he and I went to the boxing matches at the City Auditorium and watched boys from Havre fight boys from Glasgow, and afterward in the street outside we could each see the night glow of the fires, pale in the clouds just as it had been in the summer. And my father said, 'It could rain up in the canyons now, but the fire wouldn't go out. It would smolder then start again.' He blinked as the boxing crowd shoved around us. 'But here we are,' he said, and smiled, 'safe in Great Falls.'

It was during this time that my mother began to look for a job. She left an application at the school board. She worked two days at a dress shop, then quit. 'I'm lacking in powerful and influential friends,' she said to me as if it was a joke. Though it was true that we did not know anyone in Great Falls. My mother knew the people at the grocery store and the druggist's, and my father had known people at the Wheatland Club. But none of them ever came to our house. I think we might've gone someplace new earlier in their life, just picked up and moved away. But no one mentioned that. There was a sense that we were all waiting for something. Out of doors, the trees were through with turning yellow and leaves were dropping onto the cars parked at the curb. It was my first autumn in Montana, and it seemed to me that in our neighborhood the trees looked like an eastern state would and not at all the way I'd thought Montana would be. No trees is what I'd expected, only open prairie, the land and sky joining almost out of sight.

'I could get a job teaching swimming,' my mother said to me on a morning when my father left early and I was looking through the house for my school books. She was standing drinking coffee, looking out the front window, dressed in her yellow bathrobe. 'A lady at the Red Cross said I could teach privately if I'd teach a class, too.' She smiled at me and crossed her arms. 'I'm still a lifesaver.'

'That sounds good,' I said.

'I could teach your dad the backstroke again,' she said. My mother had taught me to swim, and she was good at that. She had tried to teach my father the backstroke when we lived in Lewiston, but he had tried and failed at it, and she had made a joke about it afterward. 'The lady said people want to swim in Montana. Why do you think that is? These things always signify a meaning.'

'What does it mean?' I said, holding my school books.

She hugged her arms and turned herself a little back and forth as she stood in the window frame watching out. 'Oh, that we're all going to be washed away in a big flood. Though I don't believe that. So. Some of us will *not* be washed away and will float to the top. That's better, isn't it?' She took a drink of coffee.

'It should have a happy ending for the right people,' I said.

'That's easy,' she said. 'Everyone doesn't do it that way, though.' She turned and walked back into the kitchen then to start my breakfast before school.

In the days after that, my mother went to work at the YWCA in Great Falls, at the brick building on Second Street North, near the courthouse. She walked to work from our house and carried her swimming suit in a vanity case, with a lunch to eat and some makeup articles for when she came home in the afternoon. My father said he was glad if she wanted to work there, and that I should find a job, too, which I had not done. But he didn't mention himself working or how he was spending his days or what he thought about our future or any plans he had made for things. He seemed out of reach to me, as if he had discovered a secret he didn't want to tell. Once, when I walked home from football practice, I saw him inside the Jack 'n Jill cafe, sitting at the counter drinking coffee and eating a piece of pie. He was wearing a red plaid shirt and a knitted cap, and he hadn't shaved. A man I didn't know was sitting on a stool beside him, reading the *Tribune*. They seemed to be together. Another time, on a day when the wind was blowing hard, I saw him walking away from the courthouse wearing a woolen jacket and carrying a book. He turned the corner at the library and disappeared, and I did not follow him. And one other time I saw him go into a bar called the Pheasant Lounge where I thought Great Falls city policemen went. This was at noon, and I was on my lunch hour and couldn't stay to see more.

When I told my mother that I had seen him these times she said, 'He just hasn't had a chance to get established yet. This will be all right finally. There's no lack in him.'

But I did not think things were all right. I don't believe my mother knew more than I did then. She was simply surprised, and she trusted him and thought she could wait longer. But I wondered if my parents had had troubles that I didn't know about, or if they had always had their heads turned slightly away from each other and I hadn't noticed. I know that when they shut the door to their bedroom at night and I was in my bed waiting for sleep, listening to the wind come up, I would hear their door open and close quietly, and my mother come out and make a bed for herself on the couch in the living room. Once I heard my father say, as she was leaving, 'You've changed your thinking now, haven't you, Jean?' And my mother say, 'No.' But then the door closed and she did not say anything else. I do not think I was supposed to know about this, and I don't know what they could've said to each other or done during that time. There was never yelling or arguing involved in it. They simply did not stay together at night, although during the day when I was present and life needed to go on normally there was nothing to notice between them. Coming and going was all. Nothing to make you think there was trouble or misunderstanding. I simply know there was, and that my mother for her own reasons began to move away from my father then.

After a time I quit playing football. I wanted to find a job, though I thought that when spring came, if we were still in Great Falls, I would try to throw the javelin as my father had said. I had taken the book, *Track and Field for Young Champions*, out of the library, and had found the equipment cage in the school basement and inspected the two wooden javelins there, where they were stored against the concrete wall in the shadows. They were slick and polished and thicker than I thought they'd be. Though when I picked one up, it was light and seemed to me perfect for the use it had. And I thought that I would be able to throw it, and that it might be a skill – even if it was a peculiar one – that I might someday excel at in a way my father would like.

I had not made friends in Great Falls. The boys on the football team lived farther downtown and across the river in Black Eagle. I had had friends in Lewiston, in particular a girlfriend named Iris, who went to the Catholic school and who I had exchanged letters with for several weeks when we had come to Great Falls in the spring. But she had gone to Seattle for the summer and had not written to me. Her father was an Army officer, and it could be her family had moved. I had not thought about her in a while, did not care about her really. It should've been a time when I cared about more things – a new girlfriend, or books – or when I had an idea of some kind. But I only cared about my mother and my father then, and in the time since then I have realized that we were not a family who ever cared about much more than that.

The job I found was in the photographer's studio on Third Avenue. It was a place that took airmen's photographs, and engagement and class pictures, and what I did was clean up when school was over, replace bulbs in the photographer's lamps, and rearrange the backdrops and posing furniture for the next day.

I finished with that work by five o'clock, and sometimes I would walk home past the YWCA and slip through the back door and down into the long tiled pool room where my mother taught her classes of adults until five, and from five to six was free to teach privately and be paid for it. I would stand at the far end behind the tiers of empty bleachers and watch her, hear her voice, which seemed happy and lively, encouraging and giving instruction. She would stand on the side in her black bathing suit, her skin pale, and make swimming motions with her arms for her students standing in the shallow water. Mostly they were old women, and old men with speckled bald heads. From time to time they ducked their faces into the water and made the swimming motions my mother made – slow, jerky grasps – without really swimming or ever moving, just staying still, standing and pretending. 'It's so easy,' I would hear my mother say in her bright voice, her arms working the thick air as she talked. 'Don't be afraid of it. It's all fun. Think about all you've missed.' She'd smile at them when their faces were up, dripping and blinking, some of them coughing. And she would say, 'Watch me now.' Then she'd pull down her bathing cap, point her hands over her head to a peak, bend her knees and dive straight in, coasting for a moment, then breaking the surface and swimming with her arms bent and her fingers together, cutting the water in easy reaching motions to the far side and back again. The old people – ranchers, I thought, and the divorced wives of farmers – watched her in envy and silence. And I watched, thinking as I did that someone else who saw my mother, not me or my father, but someone who had never seen her before, would think something different. They would think: 'Here is a woman whose life is happy'; or 'Here is a woman with a nice figure to her credit'; or 'Here is a woman I wish I could know better, though I never will.' And I thought to myself that my father was not a stupid man, and that love was permanent, even though sometimes it seemed to recede and leave no trace at all.

*　　　*　　　*

On the first Tuesday in October, the day before the World Series began, my father came back to the house after dark. It was chill and dry outside, and when he came in the back door his eyes were bright and his face was flushed and he seemed as if he had been running.

'Look who's here now,' my mother said, though in a nice way. She was cutting tomatoes at the sink board and looked around at him and smiled.

'I've got to pack a bag,' my father said. 'I won't have dinner here tonight, Jean.' He went straight back to their room. I was sitting beside the radio waiting to turn on some baseball news, and I could hear him opening a closet door and shoving coat hangers.

My mother looked at me, then she spoke toward the hallway in a calm voice. 'Where are you going, Jerry?' She was holding a paring knife in her hand.

'I'm going to that fire,' my father said loudly from the bedroom. He was excited. 'I've been waiting for my chance. I just heard thirty minutes ago that there's a place. I know it's unexpected.'

'Do you know anything about fires?' My mother kept watching the empty doorway as if my father was standing in it. 'I know about them,' she said. 'My father was an estimator. Do you remember that?'

'I had to make some contacts in town,' my father said. I knew he was sitting on the bed putting on different shoes. The overhead light was on and his bag was out. 'It's not easy to get this job.'

'Did you hear me?' my mother said. She had an impatient look on her face. 'I said you don't know anything about fires. You'll get burned up.' She looked at the back door, which he'd left partway open, but she didn't go to close it.

'I've been reading about fires in the library,' my father said. He came down the hall and went into the bathroom, where he turned on the light and opened the medicine cabinet. 'I think I know enough not to get killed.'

'Could you have said something to me about this?' my mother said.

I heard the medicine cabinet close and my father stepped into the kitchen doorway. He looked different. He looked like he was sure that he was right.

'I should've done that,' he said. 'I just didn't.' He had his shaving bag in his hand.

'You're not going out there.' My mother looked at my father across the kitchen, across over my head in fact, and seemed to smile. 'This is a stupid idea,' she said, and shook her head.

'No it's not,' my father said.

'It isn't your business,' my mother said, and pulled up the front of her blue apron and wiped her hands on it, though I don't think her hands were wet. She was nervous. 'You don't have to do this. I'm working now.'

'I know you are,' my father said. He turned and went back into the bedroom. I wanted to move from where I was but I didn't know where a better place was to be, because I wanted to hear what they would say. 'We're going to dig firebreaks up there,' he said from the bedroom. I heard the locks on his bag snap closed. He appeared again in the doorway, holding a gladstone bag, a bag his father had given him when he had gone away to college. 'You're not in any danger,' he said.

'I might die while you're gone,' my mother said. She sat down at the metal table and stared at him. She was angry. Her mouth looked hardened. 'You have a son here,' she said.

'This won't be for very long,' my father said. 'It'll snow pretty soon, and that'll be that.' He looked at me. 'What do you think, Joe? Is this a bad idea?'

'No,' I said. And I said it too fast, without thinking what it meant to my mother.

'You'd do it, wouldn't you?' my father said.

'Will you like it if your father gets burned up out there, and you never see him again?' my mother said to me. 'Then you and I go straight to hell together. How will that be?'

'Don't say that, Jean,' my father said. He put his bag on the kitchen table and came and knelt beside my mother and tried to put his arms around her. But she got up from her chair and walked back to where she had been cutting tomatoes and picked up the knife and pointed it at him, where he was still kneeling beside the empty chair.

'I'm a grown woman,' she said, and she was very angry now. 'Why don't you act like a grown man, Jerry?'

'You can't explain everything,' my father said.

'I can explain everything,' my mother said. She put the knife down and walked out the kitchen door and into the bedroom, the one she had not been sleeping in with my father, and closed the door behind her.

My father looked at me from where he was, still beside her chair. 'I guess my judgment's no good now,' he said. 'Is that what you think, Joe?'

'No,' I said. 'I think it is.'

And I thought his judgment was good, and that going to fight the fire was a good idea even though he might go and get killed because he knew nothing about it. But I did not want to say all of that to him because of how it would make him feel.

My father and I walked from home in the dark down to the Masonic Temple on Central. A yellow Cascade County school bus was parked at the corner of Ninth, and men were standing in groups waiting to go. Some of the men were bums. I could tell by their shoes and their coats. Though some were just regular men who were out of work, I thought, from other jobs. Three women who were going waited together under the streetlight. And inside the bus, in the dark, I could see Indians were in some of the seats. I could see their round faces, their slick hair, the tint of light off their eyeglasses in the darkness. No one would get in with them, and some men were drinking. I could smell whiskey in the night air.

My father put his bag on a stack of bags beside the bus, then came and stood next to me. Inside the Masonic Temple – which had high steps up to a glass center door – all the lights were on. Several men inside were looking out. One, who was the man I had seen with my father in the Jack 'n Jill, held a clipboard and was talking to an Indian man beside him. My father gestured to him.

'People categorize other people,' my father said. 'But you shouldn't do that. They should teach you that in school.'

I looked at the men around me. Most of them were not dressed warmly enough and were shifting from foot to foot. They looked like men used to work, though they did not seem glad to be going to fight a fire at night. None of them looked like my father, who seemed eager.

'What will you do out there?' I said.

'Work on a fire line,' my father said. 'They dig trenches the fire won't cross. I don't know much more, to tell you the truth.' He put his hands in his jacket pockets and blew down into his shirt. 'I've got this hum in my head now. I need to do something about it.'

'I understand,' I said.

'Tell your mother I didn't mean to make her mad.'

'I will,' I said.

'We don't want to wake up in our coffins, though, do we? That'd be a rude surprise.' He put a hand on my shoulder and pulled me close to him and squeezed me and laughed an odd little laugh, as if the idea had actually given him a scare. He looked across Central Avenue at the Pheasant Lounge, the place I had seen him go into the week before. On the red neon sign over the door a big cock pheasant was busting up into the night air, its wings stretched into the

33

darkness—escaping. Some men waiting at the Masonic Temple had begun to go across the street into the bar. 'I'm only thinking about right this minute now,' he said. He squeezed my shoulder again, then put his hands back into his jacket pockets. 'Aren't you cold?'

'I'm a little cold,' I said.

'Then go back home,' he said. 'You don't need to watch me get on a bus. It might be a long time. Your mother's probably thinking about you.'

'All right,' I said.

'She doesn't need to get mad at you. She's mad enough at me.'

I looked at my father. I tried to see his face in the street-light. He was smiling and looking at me, and I think he was happy for that moment, happy for me to be with him, happy that he was going to a fire now to risk whatever he cared about risking. It seemed strange to me, though, that he could be a man who played golf for a living and then one day become a man who fought forest fires. But it's what was happening, and I thought I would get used to it.

'Are you too old now to give your old dad a kiss?' my father said. 'Men love each other, too. You know that, don't you?'

'Yes,' I said. And he took my cheeks in his hands and kissed me on the mouth, and squeezed my face. His breath smelled sweet to me and his face was rough.

'Don't let what your parents do disappoint you,' he said.

'All right,' I said, 'I won't.' I felt afraid then for some reason, and I thought if I stayed there I would show him that I was, so I turned around and started back up Central in the dark and the growing cold. When I got to the corner I turned to wave good-bye. But my father was not in sight, and I thought that he had already gotten onto the bus and was waiting in his seat among the Indians.

WHEN I GOT HOME the lights were still on in our house. My mother was watching television in her bedroom, still dressed, and drinking a glass of beer. When I came in the door she looked at me as if I was my father and whatever she thought about him she thought about me, too.

'Is he gone off to fight the big fire now?' she said. She was almost casual in the way she said this. She reached and put down her glass on the bed table.

'He got on a bus,' I said.

'Just like a school-boy,' she said. She looked at her glass of beer.

'He told me he hadn't intended to cause any trouble.'

'I'm sure it's true,' my mother said. 'He has very beautiful intentions. What's your opinion?'

'I think it's all right,' I said.

My mother reached for her glass and took a drink out of

it and shook her head while she swallowed. 'What about me?' she said, and rested her glass on her stomach. People on the television were laughing. A fat man was running around a small man and being chased by a dog. I didn't feel comfortable being in the room at that moment. 'Maybe he's going to leave me. Maybe we're on our own right now.'

'I don't think he's going to do that,' I said.

'We haven't been very intimate lately. You might as well hear that.'

I did not say anything.

'You probably think I'm making too big a deal out of this, don't you?'

'I don't know what you're thinking,' I said.

'Nobody really wants to please you, that's all.' She shook her head as if it was almost a joke. 'That's all. They want to please themselves. If you're happy with that, then everything's great. If you aren't, too bad. That's important,' my mother said. 'It's the key to everything.' She put her head back on the pillow and stared up at the light globe in the ceiling. 'Happiness. Sadness. The works. You're happy if—'

Just at that moment the phone started to ring in the kitchen. I turned to go answer it, but my mother said, 'Let's don't answer that.' The phone kept ringing, loud and with a hard metal sound where it sat on the table, as if something urgent was waiting to be said by whoever was calling. But we were not going to hear it. I must've looked nervous because my mother smiled at me, a smile she had smiled at me all my life. 'Who do you think it is?' she said. The phone quit ringing and the house was completely silent except for the TV.

'Maybe it was Dad,' I said.

'Maybe it was,' she said.

'It could've been a wrong number, too,' I said, though I thought the phone call was my father and I felt afraid because I hadn't answered it.

'We'll never know now,' my mother said. 'But. What I

was saying.' She took a last drink of her beer. 'You're happy if the thing you naturally want makes the other person happy. If it's not that way, then I don't know. I guess you're in limbo.'

'Where's that?' I said, because I had never heard that word before.

'Oh,' she said. 'It's the place where nobody wants to be. It's the middle where you can't feel the sides and nothing happens. Like now.'

For a moment I felt the phone was about to start ringing again, felt a current go through the lines of the house, as if the lines were part of me, alive and surging with a message. But it didn't ring, and the feeling in me died out.

'Tomorrow might be a better day,' my mother said. 'Now's not so hot.' She reached and turned off the lamp beside her bed. 'Turn off my light, Joe,' she said. I switched off the overhead light. 'And go to bed, too,' she said, lying there in her clothes in the light from the television. 'Something'll happen to make things seem different.'

'I hope so,' I said.

My mother turned over and faced the wall. I thought she went to sleep at that instant, because she didn't say anything else to me. And I went to my room down the hall, and in a short time afterward I went to sleep myself.

The next day I went to school as I would on any other day, but my mother told me as I was leaving that she was going out that morning to look for a better job than teaching swimming classes.

'I don't want to be poor,' she said. She was standing at the bathroom sink in her petticoat, putting black pins in her hair. 'We might have to move into a smaller place,' she said. 'I thought of that. Would you mind that?'

'I think Dad will be back,' I said.

'Do you?' she said. 'Is that your best opinion on the subject?' She looked at me where I was in the hall, holding my coat and my school books under my arm. It was warm in the house. The bathroom heater was turned up high, and I could see the little blue flames.

'Yes,' I said. 'It is.' I was surprised she was thinking about these changes already.

'Fine. I'll remember that,' she said. 'Thank you.' She glanced at me with pins in her mouth and her hands in her hair, and nodded. 'You're a very trusting boy. You wouldn't be a very good lawyer. You don't want to be a lawyer, though, do you?'

'No,' I said.

'What *do* you want to be?'

This was something we had not precisely talked about for a long time, and I did not have my answer ready. 'I'd like to work on a railroad someplace,' I said.

'That's not very good,' my mother said. 'You have to find a better profession. When you come back today have a better answer.' My mother looked at herself in the mirror. 'We went to college,' she said. 'Your father and I both. But you wouldn't know it.' She stared at herself, wrinkled her nose. 'Handsome is as handsome does, I guess,' she said. 'You're wasting your life standing here watching me, sweetheart. Go to school.' And I went to school just as she said.

When I came back home at three o'clock – it was not a day that I worked at the photographer's studio – there was a car parked across the street from our house, a pink, four-door Oldsmobile I did not know, and a man was in our living room, a man I did not know either.

The man stood up when I came in the front door. He and my mother had been sitting in chairs, not very close together. My mother's hair was fixed with the black pins she had been putting in that morning, and the man had on a suit and a tie. It was still warm in the house and they were both

38

drinking bottles of beer. My mother had her shoes off and was in her stocking feet.

'Why, hello Joe,' she said. She seemed surprised. She smiled up at me and did not look at the man who was in the room with her. 'I guess you didn't work today.' She moved her hand toward the man to point him out. 'This is Mr Miller. This is my son, Joe Brinson, Warren.'

'I already know Joe,' the man said. He stepped toward me with his hand out, and I saw that he had a limp in his leg, not a bad one, just a limp that made him pull to one side the way it would if one leg was shorter than the other. It was his left leg he limped toward, and it did not seem to hurt him because he smiled when he shook my hand. He was a tall, bulky man who wore glasses, and he was older than my father—fifty maybe. His hair was thin and combed straight back on his head. He looked like someone I'd seen before but couldn't remember. I didn't think I'd ever heard his name. Warren Miller.

When Warren Miller had my hand in his own big hand, he held it for a moment as though he wanted me to know he meant it. His skin was warm and he had a big ring on, a gold ring with a red stone. He was wearing shiny black cowboy boots.

'I'm happy to see you, son,' he said. I could smell him, smell something like tobacco and hair oil on his clothes.

'I'm happy to see you,' I said.

'Where do you know Joe from?' my mother said, still smiling. She looked at me and winked.

'I know his father,' Warren Miller said. He stood back and put his hands on his hips so that his coat pushed back and showed his big chest. His skin was very pale and he was over six feet. He seemed to be inspecting me. 'His father's a hell of a golfer. I played with him at the Wheatland Club on two occasions, and he parted us all from our money. Joe was there waiting for him.'

'Do you remember that time, Joe?' my mother said.

'Yes,' I said. But I didn't remember. Warren Miller was looking at me as though he knew I didn't remember.

'Now your father's out fighting this fire, is that right?' Warren Miller said. He smiled as if there was something he liked about that. He kept his big hands on his hips.

'Yes,' I said, 'he is.'

'That's what he told *us*,' my mother said.

'Well. That's wonderful,' Warren Miller said. 'That's very good. Do you wish you could go out and fight it yourself? You probably do.'

'Yes sir,' I said.

'I think he actually does, Warren, as crazy as it seems,' my mother said, still seated, looking up at us. 'He and his dad think alike about most things these days.'

'There's not enough around to kill us, I guess,' Warren Miller said. 'I've felt that way. Men understand that.'

'Men don't understand much,' my mother said. 'It's not their long suit. They don't wake up crying, either. Women take care of that.'

'I never heard that before,' Warren Miller said, 'have you, Joe? I've waked up crying plenty of times. Songjin was a place I did that.' He looked around at my mother. I think he wanted to say something more about this subject, but all he said was, 'Korea.'

'Warren's borrowing a book from me, Joe,' my mother said, and she got up. 'I'll go get it right now.' She went back into the bedroom. She kept her books stacked on the floor of the closet behind her shoes.

'That's correct,' Warren Miller said, and I guess he was talking about the book then. He looked back at me. 'Sometimes you have to do the wrong thing just to know you're alive,' he said, but in a soft voice, a voice I didn't think he wanted my mother to hear.

'I understand,' I said, because I did understand that. I thought it was what my father had been talking about the night before, standing in the dark waiting to get on the bus.

'Everybody doesn't know that,' Warren Miller said. 'I can guarantee you that much.' He reached down in his pants pocket and came up with something he held in his big hand. 'Let me give you a present, Joe,' he said. When he opened his hand there was a small knife in it, a slender clasp knife made of silver. On the side of the case in tiny blocked letters, it said BURMA-1943. 'Some trouble isn't worth getting into, though,' he said. 'This'll remind you which to choose.'

'Thank you,' I said. I took the knife, which was warm and hard and heavier than I thought it would be. I felt for a moment that I shouldn't be taking it. Only I wanted it, and I liked Warren Miller for giving it to me. I knew he would not tell my mother about it, and neither would I.

'People do everything eventually, I guess,' I heard my mother say from the other room. I heard the closet door close and her footsteps on the floor. She appeared in the door to the hall. 'Did you hear what I said?' She had a small book in her hand, and she was smiling. 'Are you two plotting against me?' she said.

'We're shooting the breeze,' Warren Miller said. I let the silver knife slip into my pocket.

'I hope so,' my mother said. 'Here.' She held the book out to him. 'From my private library. Ex Libris Jeanette,' she said.

'What is it?' Warren Miller said. He took the book and looked at its cover, which was dark blue.

'It's what you asked me for,' my mother said. 'The selected poems of William Wordsworth. "Getting and spending we lay waste all our powers." That's what I remember.'

'I remember that,' Warren Miller said. He held the book in both his hands and looked down at the cover.

'I taught Mr Miller how to swim recently,' my mother said. 'Now he'd like to learn to read poetry.' She smiled at him and sat back down in her armchair. 'He's going to give me a job in his grain elevator, too,' she said.

'I am,' Warren Miller said. 'That's right.'

'Mr Miller owns a grain elevator,' my mother said. 'He has three of them, actually. I bet you've seen them, sweetheart.' She looked around toward the back of our house and pointed her arm over behind her head. 'They're across the river. Those big white ones. They're what we have as a skyline out here. They're probably full of oats, like Warren.'

'What *is* in them.' I asked.

'Wheat,' Warren Miller said. 'Though this isn't a good year for it. It's too hot.'

'It's too dry,' my mother said, 'in case we didn't notice. That's why we have big fires now.'

'That's correct,' Warren Miller said, and he looked uncomfortable. He kept the slender book in one hand and moved closer to the front door. It gave me an odd feeling that he was here, and that he was in his fifties and knew my mother. I tried to think about him wearing a bathing suit. 'I've got to see a man about a dog,' he said. He put his hand with the big gold and red ring on my shoulder. I could feel it on my shoulder bone. 'I'm glad I saw you, Joe,' he said.

'I'm glad you did, too,' my mother said. She didn't get up. She seemed strange, as if something had affected her and she wanted to pretend it hadn't.

'Come to see me tomorrow, Jeanette. All right?' Warren Miller said. He limped when he moved toward the door.

'All right,' my mother said, 'I will. Joe, open the door for Mr Miller.'

And I did that, with my school books in my hand and the silver knife he had given me in my pocket.

'I hope I'll see you again,' Warren Miller said to me.

'You probably will,' my mother said.

We watched Warren Miller as he limped down our front

42

steps and out past the wooden gate to his Oldsmobile, parked in the dry leaves across the street.

'He's a nice man,' my mother said, sitting and looking at me when I had shut the door. 'Doesn't he seem nice to you?'

'He does all right.'

'He can swim very nicely. You'd be surprised – for a big man. He fought in two wars but never learned to swim. Isn't that odd? You're not supposed to be able to do that.' She looked up at the ceiling as if she was thinking about it. 'I said I could explain everything, didn't I? But I can't.'

I looked out the front window at the Oldsmobile, which was parked where it had been. Warren Miller was sitting in the driver's seat looking at our house. I lifted my hand and waved at him. But he couldn't see me. He sat there and looked for a time longer, then he started the car and drove away.

At five o'clock my mother came into my room where I was setting out a problem for my geometry class in school. She had taken a nap after Warren Miller had left, and then taken a bath and talked on the phone. When she came in my room she was dressed in a way that was new to me. She had on blue jeans and a white western shirt and some blue-colored cowboy boots I had known her to have but had never seen her wear. She had a red kerchief around her neck, tied in a knot.

'Do you like this particular get-up?' she said, and looked down at the toes of her boots.

'It looks nice,' I said.

'Thank you very much.' She looked at herself in the mirror over my chest of drawers, across the room. 'I used to dress like this all the time in eastern Washington,' she said. 'In the last century.' She took hold of the doorknob and

43

turned it gently as she stood there. 'I used to stand behind the bull chutes at the rodeos and hope some cowboy would approve of me. It made my father very mad. He wanted me to go to college, which is where I did go. And where I want you to go, incidentally.'

'I want to go,' I said. I had given some thought to that, already, but I hadn't thought about a profession yet. I hoped she wouldn't ask me about that again for a while.

'Southern Cal's very good,' my mother said. She looked out my window, stooping a little as if she wanted to see out toward the west. 'That's where I want you to go. Or Harvard. They're both good schools.'

'I'd go there,' I said. I didn't know where either of these schools was located or why they were good. I'd only heard their names before.

'I've never taken you to the rodeos, I guess,' she said. 'I'm sorry.' She was leaning against the door to my room, looking at me lying on the bed with my books and papers. She was thinking about something that had nothing to do with me, I thought. Maybe she was thinking about my father. 'Western boys are supposed to go to rodeos. However. I used to race barrels in Briscoe. I certainly did do that. Against other girls. And I wore this get-up. I did it for the sole and simple reason of attracting attention to myself. They used to call us chute beauties. Isn't that interesting? Isn't that an impressive thing to know about your mother? That she was a chute beauty?'

'Dad told me about that,' I said. 'He likes it.'

'Did he? Does he? That's good. It's probably nice to know your parents were once not your parents. It seems merciful to me at this moment.'

'I knew that, too,' I said.

'Well, good for you,' my mother said. She walked around my bed and stood looking out the window, across our sunny yard toward the river and the oil refinery, and farther away toward the hazy sky behind which was the fire my father was fighting. 'Would you like to take a drive?' she said, putting her fingers on the glass as though she wanted to push it. 'I'd like to see the fire. I think you can drive right to where it is. I read that in the paper. You can consider it the beginning of your higher education.'

'I'd like to see it,' I said, and closed my geometry book.

'Maybe we'll see something astounding that you'll always remember,' my mother said, her fingers still on the window glass. 'That certainly doesn't happen every day. At least not at my age it doesn't. Although maybe at your age it does.'

'How old are you,' I asked because I realized I did not know how old she or my father was.

'Thirty-seven,' my mother said, and looked at me sharply. 'Does that seem like the wrong age? Would you like it better if I said fifty? Would that make you feel better?'

'No,' I said. 'Thirty-seven's all right.'

'Don't you feel protected enough?'

'I haven't thought about that, I guess,' I said.

'I won't be this age forever,' she said, 'so don't start. It'd just confuse you.' She smiled and shook her head. I thought she was going to laugh, but she didn't laugh. She just walked out of the room and off into her own bedroom to get ready to go.

We drove in our family Plymouth from Great Falls, west along the Sun River and Route 200, out through the towns of Vaughn and Simms and Fort Shaw and Sun River itself, towns on the bottom edge of the wheat land beyond which were the large mountains. The light that evening was clear autumn light, and everything – the stubble, the witch grass edges, the cottonwood flats below the Fairfield bench – was gold and dry, the color of the sun. Ducks were in the river eddies, and now and then I could see a farmer cutting silage

45

rows through his corn stand. It seemed to me an odd time for a fire to go on. Though out ahead of us, beyond the town of Augusta where the mountains commenced, smoke rose like a screen that drifted northward up the front to Canada, thick and white at the bottom but thinner and drifting above, so that as my mother drove us closer and the peaks became hidden by smoke, it came to seem that there were no mountains, and where the dense smoke began the plains and even the world itself came to an end.

'Do you know what they call trees in a forest fire,' my mother asked as she drove through Augusta, where there were only a few buildings—a hotel and some red bar signs, a service station—and a few people on the sidewalk.

'What?' I said.

'Fuel. Trees are fuel. A fox fleeing from a flaming fuel-fed forest fire. Did you ever hear that?'

'No,' I said.

'It was just a funny joke when I was in college,' she said. 'Do you know what they call the trees that're left up when the fire goes by?'

'No,' I said.

'The standing dead,' my mother said. 'Don't they have an interesting terminology for things? My father told me all about it. He felt it was broadening.'

'What happens to the animals,' I asked.

'Oh, they adjust, though the little ones have a hard time. They get confused. Everything happens before they know it. I used to cry about it, but my father said it didn't help anything. He was right.'

We drove through Augusta and out onto a dirt road that crossed a creek bottom, then went up into the white smoke. It was going nearer to dark then, and the sun was whitish behind the smoke, and north and south of us the evening sky was red and purple.

The fire was out ahead, though we couldn't see flames yet. Along the way, a few cars were stopped on the roadside and people were standing in the grass or sitting on their car hoods, watching with binoculars or taking pictures. Some had out-of-state tags, and some people were holding flashlights. A few of the cars that had started back had their headlights on.

'It's a sickening smell,' my mother said, and cleared her throat. I didn't know if she knew where we were going. She was just driving into the smoke. 'People get drawn to it. They don't want it to be over.'

'Why?' I said, watching up onto the hillside. As the creek bottom grew narrower, I could see small individual yellow fires and longer lines of fire in the dark with barely distinguishable human figures moving in the trees.

'Oh, I guess.' My mother seemed annoyed. 'I guess they think something worse is happening someplace else, so they're better off with a tragedy they already know. It's not a generous thought.'

'Maybe that's not right,' I said. And I thought that because I didn't see what any of this had to do with my father.

'Maybe not,' my mother said, 'maybe you're smart and I'm stupid.'

'Do you like Miller?' I said. I had wanted to know it in the afternoon, but there hadn't seemed enough reason to ask, whereas now for some reason there did.

'Do you mean Mr Miller? Warren?' my mother said.

'Yes,' I said. 'Do you like him?'

'Not very much,' she said. 'Things do happen around him, though. He has that feel about him, doesn't he?'

'I don't know,' I said. I had the knife he had given me in my pocket, a thing he had given me to make me like him. But that was all that had happened to me where Warren Miller was concerned.

'He's going to give me a job to keep his books at his grain elevator,' my mother said. 'That's something. And he's asked you and me to have supper at his house tomorrow

47

night. Which is lucky because I had plans to open up some cans. Why?'

'I was interested,' I said. The truth was I wanted to know what she thought about my father leaving, and I hoped this would get around to that subject. Though it didn't, and I didn't know how to make it.

'It's always just yourself,' my mother said. 'Nothing else.'

'What does that mean?' I said.

'Honey, nothing. I was thinking and talking. It's a bad habit. You have an inquiring intelligence. Everything will always surprise you. You'll have a wonderful life.' She smiled.

'Don't they surprise you?'

'Not much,' my mother said. 'Now and then I run upon the unexpected. But that's all. Look up there now, Joe.'

Ahead of us at the end of the canyon, the creek bottom road opened into a wide grass meadow beyond which a hill went up sharply, full of small fires in sparse trees.

'Let's give you the full treatment,' my mother said, and she stopped the car right there, still in the narrow canyon where there were patches of fire burning ten yards from the road. She turned off the motor. 'Open your door,' she said. 'See what it feels like.'

I opened my side and stepped out on the road just as she'd told me to. And the fire was all around me, up the hill on both sides and in front of me and behind. The small yellow fires and lines of fire were flickering in the under-brush close enough that I could've touched them just by reaching out. There was a sound like wind blowing, and a crack of limbs on fire. I could feel the heat of it all over the front of me, on my legs and my fingers. I smelled the deep, hot piny odor of trees and ground in flames. And what I wanted to do was get away from it before it overcame me.

I got back in the car with my mother and closed the door. It was instantly cooler and quieter.

'How was that?' she said, and looked at me.

48

'It's loud,' I said. My hands and legs still felt hot.

'Did it appeal to you?' my mother said.

'No,' I said, 'it scared me.' And that is the feeling I'd had when it was all around me.

'It's just a lot of small fires that once in a while blow together. Don't be afraid now,' my mother said. 'You just needed to see what your father finds so entrancing. Do you understand it?'

'No,' I said, and I thought my father might've been surprised by such a fire and want to come home.

'I don't understand either,' my mother said. 'It's not mysterious at all.'

'Maybe he was surprised,' I said.

'I'm sure he was,' my mother said. 'I'm sorry we both can't sympathize with him.' She started the car and drove us on.

In the meadow was a tent camp where there were trucks and temporary lights strung on lines between wooden poles. Fires were beside the road. Small ones. People were moving inside the camp—mostly men, I thought, brought there to fight the fire. Some I could see lying on cots inside tents that had their flaps left open. Some were standing and talking. Others were sitting in trucks. A small dark airplane with a white star on its tail section was sitting farther out in the meadow. Straight across the road that we were on and still ahead of us was a small service station where more trucks were, and a white-lighted CAFE sign hung out in the early evening darkness. We passed a sign that said that this was Truly, Montana, though it was hard to tell what made it a town. It only seemed to be a separate place because all around it a fire was burning.

'This is quite a place,' my mother said, watching out the windshield as we drove into the little town of Truly. She motioned toward the tent camp. 'That's the stage-up over there,' she said, 'where everyone leaves and comes back. It's just smoke all the time up here. You're never out of it.'

'Do you think we can drive in and find Dad?'

'No we can't,' my mother said abruptly. 'He's fresh out. They'll keep him up there till he drops. Then he'll come down, if he's alive enough. I'm not going to look for him. Are you hungry?'

'Yes,' I said. But I was watching the hillside and only half listening. I watched a tall spruce tree catch fire high in the dark. A spark had found it, and it exploded in a bright, steepling yellow flame that leaped and shot out bits of fire into the night toward other trees, and swirled its own white smoke, flaming and then dying quickly as the wind on the hillside – a wind that did not blow where we were – changed and died. It all happened in an instant, and I knew it was dangerous though in a beautiful way. And I understood, just as I sat there in the car with my mother, what I thought dangerous was: it was a thing that did not seem able to hurt you, but quickly and deceivingly would. Though I didn't understand why my father would risk danger, unless it was that he didn't care about life much, or unless there was something in losing it that was satisfying, which didn't seem like anything I remembered anybody ever having said to me.

In the cafe we sat in a booth by the window so we could both see across the road to the fire camp and the fire itself, which turned the sky red above the ridge lines so that you knew that beyond where you could see there was more fire and men fighting it.

My mother ordered fried chicken for both of us, and as we sat waiting, a truck stopped in front of the cafe, and fifteen or so men got off the back of it, wearing heavy canvas clothing and boots, their faces blackened with fire soot, and moving as if they were stiff and tired. The men were all big men with heavy gaits and they all came inside the cafe together and sat at four of the tables without talking. The two women who were the waitresses went around the tables asking if the men wanted what they usually had – fried steaks and potatoes – and they all said yes, then sat drinking their water and talking softly while they waited. They were young men – older than I was, but still young. And there was a smell that came from them and went all through the room. The smell of cold ashes, a smell that came right out of their clothes and stayed in the air, as if the men had just walked right out of the fire itself and had been burned by it and this was what was left of them.

My mother had glanced at the men when they sat down, then looked back out the window at the lighted stage camp beyond our car, and up onto the ridge and hillside which was on fire in small blazes like campfires. She ordered a can of beer and drank it out of the can as she stared out.

'I think it's just because he lost his job,' she said. When she said that she looked at the men who were at the tables across the room. 'It made him go crazy. I feel sorry for him. I actually do.' She looked back out the window into the night.

'He's all right,' I said, and I know I was thinking that these other men were all right. They were here eating supper, and probably my father was too, somewhere else. He was on his own, and that was all, and you did not have to be crazy to want to be on your own, or so I thought at the time.

'Is that what you believe?' my mother said, holding her beer can in both hands, her elbows on the table top.

'Yes,' I said. 'It is.'

'Well, I think he has a woman out there is what I think. Probably it's an Indian woman. A squaw. She's probably married, too.' My mother said this as if she was accusing me and I was going to have to answer for it. Something about me must've reminded her of my father. 'I read that women were out there,' she said.

'I saw some who were going,' I said. One of the men

seated at the firefighters' tables looked at my mother. She had raised her voice a little.

'Well, why do you think men do things?' my mother said. 'They either go crazy or it's a woman. Or it's both. You don't know anything. How could you? You haven't done anything.' She stared back at the man who was looking at her, and touched the red kerchief around her neck. But when she looked at me she was smiling. 'It's nature's way,' she said to me. 'That can be part of your education, to learn what nature's way is.'

'All right,' I said. Two more of the firefighters looked at us, and one of them smiled and cleared his throat. I wished I knew what nature's way was, because all that was happening in our family did not not seem to be natural or normal.

'Tell me how you feel about your name,' my mother said after a minute had passed, and in a quieter voice. 'Do you like it all right? Joe? It's not an uncommon name. We didn't want to weigh you down with a fancy name or a middle name. We liked Joe.'

'I like it,' I said. 'It's easy for people to remember.'

'That's true,' she said. She glanced back at the night. There were stars in the October sky, and somehow through the white smoke they had become visible. 'Jeanette,' she said. 'I never liked that. It seemed like a waitress's name.'

'What one would you rather have,' I asked.

'Well,' my mother said, and drank the last of her beer. Our food was coming now. I could see it in the window to the kitchen, two plates steaming, the top of a woman's head just visible behind it. 'Lottie,' my mother said, and smiled. She pushed her hair up with one hand. 'There used to be a singer named Lottie. Lottie something. Lottie-da. She was colored, I think. But. How would that be? Lottie?'

'I don't like it,' I said. 'I like Jeanette.'

'Well, that's sweet,' my mother said and smiled at me. 'You have to like me the way I am. Not as Lottie, I guess.'

Our food came and we ate it and talked about forest fires,

52

that they were like cities or factories, and went on and on by themselves. That there was something good about them, that they replenished where they burned, and that for humans, my mother said, it was sometimes a good thing to be near a thing so uncontrollable and out of all scale that you felt reduced and knew your position in the world. She understood my father in some ways, she said. He wasn't the kind to go crazy. It was only a hard time in his life, though it was a hard time in hers too. That was nature's way, also, she said. People were drawn to things they shouldn't be. I thought she seemed happy to be there with me and to see the fire, happy to have said all the things we'd said. Then we started home to Great Falls.

On the drive back, the air had become colder as we went farther east of the fire, and the sky was clear and starry except for the glow the city made low on the horizon. My mother stopped in Augusta and bought two more beers for the road and drank as she drove and did not talk to me much. I thought mostly about my father, then, and about what he would be like when he came back. He had been gone since only the night before, but already the life he left didn't seem like the same life to me, and when I pictured him coming back, I pictured him getting off the back of a truck like the men at the cafe, although he was not smudged with ashes or stiff or tired, but looked clean and younger than when he had left and did not in fact even look like himself, but like someone else. And I realized that I could not exactly remember his face or his features. I could hear the sound of his voice, but that was all. And the only face I could see was the strange young man I did not think I knew.

When we had driven back almost to Great Falls and could see down onto the city at night and could see the white grain elevators that Warren Miller owned lighted beside the river, my mother said, 'Let's go in a new way.' And instead of straight in on Central Avenue, she drove us more toward the north side so that we came down into town through Black Eagle, the way you'd come in if you'd driven down from Fort Benton and the Hi-line, and not from the west.

I didn't wonder why we'd come this way and did not bother to ask. My mother was a person who did not like doing things always the same way, and would go out of her way to make a drive we took not be dull, or some explanation not the same as it was the last time. 'Make life intriguing,' she would say when she turned off some road we knew onto an unknown one, or when she'd buy things in a store, something she had never bought and had no use for. 'Life's just small potatoes,' she'd say; 'you have to apply yourself.'

We drove down the long hill that ends at the Missouri River, beyond which is the old part of Great Falls, the part where we lived, where there are parks and tree-lined streets set out by the original builders. But two blocks before the river, my mother turned left and drove down a street of frame houses that were set up on the hillside embankment in rows, overlooking the river and the lights of town. I had been on this street before. Farther down was an Italian steakhouse where I had gone with my father once at night to eat dinner with some men from the Wheatland Club. 'A smoker,' he had called it, and only men were there. And I had always thought it was a part of town where only Italians lived.

My mother did not drive as far as the restaurant, although I could see it there on the dark street, lighted in a blue light with cars parked in front. When we'd gone two blocks, she slowed and opened the window, then stopped in front of a house that sat up above the street and had a steep concrete driveway and a set of steep steps that ran up beside it to the wooden steps of the house. The house was like the other house beside it, white and tall-fronted with one large window and a front door on one side. A light was burning on the porch, and the draperies in the window were drawn open and an old-fashioned yellow lamp sat on a table. It looked like a house where an old person would live.

My mother sat and looked up at the house for a moment, then rolled her window up.

'Whose house is that,' I asked.

'It's Warren's house,' my mother said, and sighed. 'It's Mr Miller's house.' She put her hands on top of the steering wheel but just sat looking down the street toward the restaurant.

'Are we going inside?'

'No, we're not,' she said. 'No one's home, anyway. I had something to ask Mr Miller, but it can wait.'

'Maybe they're in there,' I said.

'They're not *they*,' my mother said. 'It's just Mr Miller. He lives there alone. He had a wife but she left him, I guess. And his mother lived there, but she died.'

'When were you in there?' I said.

'I never was,' my mother said, and she seemed tired. She had driven a long way that afternoon and night, and things had not been easy for her since yesterday. 'I looked it up in the phone book, that's all,' she said. 'I should've just called. But it'll be okay now. He doesn't live like a rich man, does he? Just this plain house on a plain street.'

'No,' I said. 'He doesn't.'

'He certainly is, though,' my mother said. 'He has holdings. Those elevators. And an Oldsmobile agency. Farms. It's hard to think about.' She put the car into gear, but sat then there in the darkness as if she was trying to remember something or figure something out. 'I feel like I need to wake up,' she said, and smiled at me. 'But I don't know what from. Or to. That's a big change.' She took a deep breath and let it out, then let the car idle down the street into the night toward home. And I wondered, as we turned and started back toward the street that crossed the river, what she had needed to ask Warren Miller at nine at night, something that couldn't wait but then did. And why, since it seemed to me that someone was at home there, wouldn't she just go to the door and ask what she wanted – probably something about her job that started the next day – and then go home just as we were doing, in the regular way that people did things, the way I understood them?

IN THE MORNING my mother got up and dressed for work and left the house before I ever got out of bed. From my room, I could hear her moving around the house, her footsteps on the hard floor, and it seemed to me she was in a hurry, that maybe she did not want to see me. I stayed in bed listening until I heard the car start cold in the driveway, idle a few minutes while she came back in the house, then drive away down Eighth Street.

For a while after that I heard the furnace going on and off in the cellar, and the sound of cars passing in the street, and the sound of birds walking the eaves of our house, tapping and fluttering as distinctly as if they were in the room with me. Light was up, and the air outside my window looked clear and clean. But I felt tired. I could feel my lungs as if a weight was pressing on them, and I could hear myself breathe down in my chest and my skin felt tight. It was a sick feeling to have, and I wondered if it would go away in a day or if it was the beginning of some real illness.

For several minutes I thought I wouldn't go to school that day, that I would stay at home and sleep, or go on a walk through town as I had other times, or go to my job early or go fishing in the river. Or I thought I could walk over to the Oldsmobile agency on Tenth Avenue and have a look. No one knew me. I could ask a question or several questions of someone–about Warren Miller, about what kind of man he was; was he married, did he have children, what were his holdings? I tried to remember the day when I had met him, a day with my father at the Wheatland Club. What had he said to me? What had I said to him, if anything? What my father had said, what the weather had been like. I tried to guess whether my mother had known him for a long time or a little. Not that it mattered–any of these facts–or would change anything. They would just fill in so that if suddenly my life changed I could have something to think about.

When I'd lain in bed a while, thinking things in this way, the phone rang in the kitchen. I thought it would be my mother telling me to go to school, and I almost didn't answer it. But I did, still in my pajamas, and it was my father calling home from the fire.

'Hello, Joe,' he said to me in a loud voice. 'What's going on over there?'

'I'm going to school,' I said.

'Where's your mother? I'd like to talk to her.' The connection began to be not very good.

'She's not here,' I said. 'She went to town.'

'Is she mad at me?' he said.

'No,' I said. 'She's not.'

'I hope she's not,' he said. Then he didn't say anything for a few seconds and it sounded as though a truck was starting up behind him. I heard voices shouting, and I thought he must be calling from the restaurant where we'd been last night. 'We don't have any control over anything here now,' my father said loudly over the noise. 'We just watch everything burn. That's all. It exhausts you. I'm stiff all over from it.'

'Are you coming home,' I asked.

'I saw a bear that caught on fire, Joe,' my father said, still loud. 'You wouldn't have believed it. It just blew up around him in one instant. A live bear in a hemlock tree. I swear. He hit the ground squalling. It was like balled lightning.'

I wanted to ask about something else he'd seen, or something that had happened to him or somebody else. I wanted to ask how dangerous it was. But I was afraid I'd say the wrong thing. So all I said was, 'How do you feel?' This was a question I had never asked my father in my life. That was not the way we'd ever talked.

'I feel good,' he said. 'I feel like I've been here a year, but I've only been here a day.' Then the truck noise stopped and the connection went dim. 'Regular life doesn't exist out here,' he said. 'You have to adapt.'

'I understand,' I said.

'Is your mother already stepping out on me?' my father said, and he was joking. I was sure of that. 'I tried to call last night,' he said, 'but no one answered.'

'We ate at a cafe,' I said. 'We had chicken.'

'That's good,' my father said. 'Good for you two. I hope you were the one who paid for it.'

'She paid for us,' I said. No one had told me not to say where we had been or where my mother was. But I felt like I had a responsibility not to. Flies were crawling on the kitchen window glass where I was looking into the back yard. And I thought that the weather might be turning, and it would get colder and snow, and the fire would be out before long.

'Tell your mother that I haven't lost my mind out here yet. Okay?' There was more static on the line.

'All right,' I said. 'I will.'

I heard him laugh, then there was a click on the line, and I could hear my father say, 'Hello? Hello? Joe, where are you? Oh shoot, now.'

'Hello,' I said, 'I'm still here.' But he couldn't hear me. Something, I thought, might've burned through the line. And when I had listened a moment more to his voice, I said, 'Good-bye. Yes. Good-bye,' and said his name. And then I hung up the phone and went to dress myself for school.

That day at my school was an odd day. I remember it very clearly because I arrived late and did not have an excuse from my mother and felt tired and half in a dream, as if I hadn't slept at all or was on my way to being sick. I missed a test in my English class because I hadn't done homework from the night before. And in my civics class someone brought that day's copy of the *Tribune* and read a story aloud from it, which said there was moisture in the air now, and soon it would both rain and snow, and the fire in Allen Creek would go out. After that we had a debate on whether the fire would actually go out – some said it would burn all winter – and if man would cause it or nature would. My teacher, who was a tall half-Indian man, asked us if any of our fathers were fighting the fire, and several people put up their hands. But I didn't because I didn't want it known and because it didn't seem like a normal matter in my life then.

Sitting in my geometry class later, waiting for school to end, it seemed like a cold afternoon out of doors. I tried to think of what was between my mother and Warren Miller now, because something seemed to be. And not because of what they'd said to each other when I was present or said to me or might've said that I knew nothing about, but because of what they didn't say but just presumed, the way you presumed moisture was in the air or that there were no more degrees in a circle than three hundred and sixty.

Though whatever it was, it had been worth a lie. My mother had lied to my father, and I had too. Maybe Warren Miller had lied to someone. And while I knew very well what a lie was, I didn't know what difference it made when adults did it. Possibly it mattered less for them inasmuch as in their lives, what was and wasn't so would finally be plain for everyone to see. Whereas for me, because I had done nothing in the world to represent me, it mattered more. And as I sat at my desk in the cool October afternoon, I tried to think of a happy life for myself and a happy and gay life for my parents when all this would be over, as my mother said everything would be. But all I could think of as I sat there was my father saying, 'Hello? Hello? Joe, where are you?' And of myself saying, 'Good-bye.'

When school was over I walked to my job at the photographer's studio, and then I walked home. The weather was changing and there was a breeze blowing, the kind of windy breeze that eventually turns icy in Montana and blows through your skin as if you were made of paper. I knew the same wind would be blowing that day where the fire was burning, and that it would have consequences there. And I wondered if it might snow in the mountains and thought that it would, and that with luck my father would come home sooner than anyone thought.

When I got in our house my mother was standing at the sink in the kitchen. She was looking out toward where the sun was setting. She had on a blue and white dress that looked like a navy dress. Her hair was tied up in back in what she called a French bun. It was a way she fixed herself that I liked. She had been looking at the newspaper, which was open on the countertop.

'Winter, winter, go away,' she said, staring out the window. She looked around at me and smiled. 'You're not dressed warmly enough. Next you'll be sick. Then *I'll* be sick.' She looked back outside. 'Did you have a very enjoyable day today at school?'

'Not a very good one,' I said. 'I missed a test. I forgot.'

'Well. Do better there, then,' she said. 'Harvard only has a few places available for boys from the ends of the earth. Somebody else from Great Falls probably expects to go to Harvard, too. And they won't want to take both of you. I certainly wouldn't.'

'Where did you go so early?' I said. 'I was awake.'

'Were you really?' my mother said. 'I could've driven you to school.' She moved away from the window and began refolding the newspaper page by page. 'Oh, I went out-wards,' she said. 'I saw in this paper this morning a notice for a job teaching math to boys at the air base. Some of them can't add out there, I guess. So I filled out an application to be industrious. I have an urge to do good all of a sudden.' She finished folding the paper and pushed it neatly to the side and turned around toward me. I wanted to ask her about going to work for Warren Miller.

'Dad called this morning,' I said. 'I talked to him.'

'Where was he?' my mother said. She did not look surprised, only interested.

'I don't know. I thought he was at the fire. He didn't say where he was.'

'Where did you say I was?'

'I said you were gone to town. I thought that was right.' I did not want to tell her he had asked if she was stepping out on him. I knew she wouldn't like that.

'You thought I was gone to work for Mr Miller. Is that right?'

'Yes,' I said.

'Well, I was. Or I did. I went there and did a few things. It's just part-time. I still have a son to raise at home, I think.'

'That's okay,' I said. I was glad to hear her say that even if she was only making a joke. 'Is Miller married?' I said. And these were words that just said themselves. I hadn't planned to say them.

'I already talked about that,' my mother said. 'He was.' She walked to the refrigerator and took out an ice tray and carried that to the sink and ran water over it. 'He lived in that house with his mother and his little wife. The three of them. For quite some time, I guess. Then the old lady died–his mother. And not long after that his wife, whose name was Marie LaRose or some such thing, ran off some-where. To California or Colorado–one of those–with an oil wildcatter. Forty-six years old, and off she goes.'

My mother took a white coffee cup out of the cabinet, put one ice cube in it, then took a full bottle of Old Crow whiskey from under the sink, uncapped it, and poured some into the cup. She was talking while she did this and not looking at me. I wondered if she would tell this all to my father if he asked her, and I decided she probably wouldn't.

'Do you feel sorry for him,' I asked.

'For Warren Miller?' my mother said, and she looked at me quickly, then back at her cup on the sink top where she was stirring the ice cube with her finger. 'Indeed-ee-not. I don't feel sorry for anybody. I don't feel sorry for myself, so I don't see why I should feel sorry for these other people. In particular those I don't know very well.' She looked at me again, quickly, then lifted the cup up and leaned forward to take a sip. 'I made this too full,' she said before she tasted the whiskey, then she drank some.

'Dad said they can't control the fire out there now,' I said. 'He said they just watch it.'

'Well, then, he's perfect for that. He likes golf.' She held the cup under the faucet and let water trickle into it. 'Your father has very pretty hands, have you ever noticed them? They're like a girl's. He'll ruin them fighting forest fires. My father's hands were like big lug nuts. That's what he used to say.'

'He said he hoped you weren't still mad at him,' I said.

'He's a sweet man,' my mother said. 'I'm not mad at him. Did you two have a nice chat about me? All my character flaws on parade? Did he talk about his Indian woman he has out there?' She carried the ice tray back to the refrigerator. It was almost dark outside, and I snapped the light on in the kitchen. It was a dim light and only made the room seem small and dirty.

'Turn that off,' my mother said. She was annoyed at me for having talked about her, which I hadn't done. She took her cup of whiskey and sat down at the kitchen table. 'I went out and looked at an apartment today. I looked at those Helen Apartments over on Second. They have a two-bedroom that's nice. It's near the river and it's close to your school, too.'

'Why are we going to do that?' I said.

'Because,' my mother said. She put her ring finger through the little cup handle and looked at the cup on the table. She spoke very clearly, and in my memory very slowly. 'This fire could go on for a long time. Your father may want a new life. I don't know. I have to be smart about things. I have to think about who pays bills. I have to think about the rent here. Things are different now in case you haven't noticed. You can get drawn in over your head if you don't look out. You can lose your peace of mind.'

'I don't think that's true,' I said, because I thought my father was gone working to put out a fire, and would soon be back. My mother was going too far. She was saying the wrong words and did not even believe them herself.

'I don't mind saying that,' my mother said. 'He's not lacking. I told you that before.' She kept her finger through the cup handle, but did not lift it. She looked tense and tired and unhappy sitting there, trapped in the way she saw the world and her life – a bad way. 'Maybe we just shouldn't have moved up here,' she said. 'Maybe we should've stayed in Lewiston. You can make so many adjustments you don't know what's what anymore.' She wasn't happy to be saying these words because she did not like to rearrange things, even in her thoughts. And as far as I knew, she hadn't had to do that in her life. She raised the cup and took a drink of the whiskey. 'I suppose you think I'm the horrible one now, don't you?'

'No,' I said. 'I don't.'

'Well, that's right,' my mother said, 'I'm not. It'd be nice if somebody was in the wrong for a change. It'd make everybody feel better.'

'I wouldn't feel better,' I said.

'Okay. Then not you,' my mother said, and nodded. 'Joe chooses for his only choice in the world to do the absolutely correct best thing. Good luck to him.' She looked around at me and the expression on her face was an expression of dislike, one I hadn't seen before but knew right away. Later I would see it turned toward other people. But the first time was looking at me and was because she believed she'd done all she could that was correct and the best thing, and it had only gotten her left with me. And I couldn't do anything that mattered. Though if I could I would've had my father be there, or Warren Miller, or somebody who had the right words that would take the place of hers, anybody she could speak to without just hearing her own voice in a room and having to go to the trouble of pretending she did not feel absolutely alone.

At seven o'clock that night my mother and I drove across the river to Warren Miller's house to eat dinner with him. My mother wore a bright green dress and high heels that were the same color, and she had taken her hair down out of the French bun and put on perfume.

'This is my desperation dress,' she said to me when I was waiting for her in the living room, and where I could see her through the bathroom door in front of the mirror. 'Your father should see me wearing this,' she said, brushing her hair back with her fingers. 'He'd approve of it. Inasmuch as he paid for it.'

'He'd like it,' I said.

'Oh yes,' she said, 'I'm sure he would too.' She drank the last of her cup of whiskey and left it in the sink as we went out the back door.

In the car she was in a good humor, and I was, too, because of it. We drove through the middle of Great Falls, past the Masonic Temple where no lights were on, and past the Pheasant Lounge across Central, where the neon sign hung out dimly in the night. It was cold now, and my mother had not worn a coat and was cold herself, though she said she wanted to feel the air to get her bearings.

She drove us down to Gibson Park and along the river so that we passed the Helen Apartments, which was a long four-story redbrick building I had never seen before but where several windows were lighted and in one or two I could see someone sitting by a lamp reading a newspaper.

'How do *you* feel,' my mother asked, looking over at me. 'Out of reach? I wouldn't be surprised.'

'No,' I said. 'I feel fine.' I was looking out at the Helen Apartments as we drove past them. They did not seem like bad places to me. Maybe our life would be better there.

'Sometimes'–my mother straightened her bare arms toward the steering wheel and looked ahead toward Black Eagle, across the river–'if you can just get a little distance on your fate, things seem okay. I like that. It's a relief to me.'

'I know it,' I said, because I felt relieved just at that moment.

'Keep your distance,' she said. 'Then everybody–girls included–will think you're smart. And maybe you will be.' She reached down to turn on the radio. 'Let's have some mood music,' she said. I remember very distinctly there was a man's voice speaking in a foreign language, which I guessed was French. He was speaking very fast, and seemed very far away. 'Canada,' my mother said. 'We live near Canada now. My God.' She clicked the radio off. 'I can't stand Canada tonight,' she said. 'Sorry. We'll have Canada later.' And we turned and drove on across the Fifteenth Street Bridge and up into Black Eagle.

Warren Miller's house was the only one on his street with a porch light shining. And once we had stopped across the street from it, I could see that all the lights inside were burning, and the house–set up above the street–looked warm inside like a place where a party was going on or was ready to begin. Warren Miller's pink Oldsmobile was parked halfway up the driveway, and farther down the street I could see the blue light of the Italian steakhouse. In front of Warren's car, in the shadows beside the house, I saw there was a motorboat on a trailer, the smooth white hull pointed up.

'It's all lit up in there, isn't it?' my mother said. She seemed pleased by the lights. She turned the rearview mirror toward her and opened her eyes very wide, closed them and opened them again as if she'd been asleep. I wondered what she would say if I told her I didn't want to go in Warren Miller's house, and that I wanted to walk back home over the bridge. I thought she would make me go anyway, and this was something I had no choice in. 'Well,' she said, turning the mirror back in the dark. 'Handsome is as handsome looks, too. Are you going inside with me? You don't have to. You can go home.'

'No.' And I was surprised by that. 'I'm hungry,' I said.

'Great,' my mother said. She opened the car door onto the cold night's air, and together we got out to go inside the house.

Warren Miller opened the front door before we were all the way up the front steps. He had a white dish towel tucked inside his belt front like an apron. He was wearing a white shirt, suit pants and cowboy boots, and he was smiling, not so much in a happy way as in a serious one. He seemed older to me and bigger than he had the day before, and his limp seemed worse. His eyeglasses were shining and his thin black hair was slicked back and gleaming. He was not handsome at all, and did not look like a man who read poetry or played golf or who had a lot of money or holdings. But I knew those things were all true.

'You look like a beauty pageant queen, Jeanette,' he said to my mother on the steps. He talked loudly, much louder than he had the day before. He was framed in the lighted doorway, and inside the house on a table by the door, I could see a glass he had been drinking out of.

'I was–on one occasion,' my mother answered. And she walked right by him through the door. 'Where's the heater in here? I'm frozen,' I heard her say, then she disappeared inside.

'You have to say the nice things to women,' Warren Miller said to me, and he put his large hand on my shoulder again. We were in the doorway, and I could smell whatever he was drinking on his breath. 'Do you always say them to your mother?'

'Yes sir,' I said. 'I try to.'

'Are you looking after her welfare?' I could hear him breathe down in his chest. His eyes were watery blue behind his glasses.

'Yes,' I said. 'I do that.'

'You can't trust anybody.' He gripped my shoulder hard. 'You can't even trust yourself. You're no damn good, are you? I can tell. I'm part Indian.' He laughed when he said that.

'No,' I said. 'I guess I'm not.' And I laughed, too. Then, holding my shoulder, he pushed me through the door and into the house.

Inside, the air was very warm and thick with cooking smells. Every light I could see was turned on, and the doors to all the rooms were open so that from the middle of the living room you could see into two bedrooms where there were double beds and, farther on, into a bathroom that had white tiles. Everything in the house was neat and clean, and everything seemed old-fashioned to me. The wallpaper had pale orange flowers in it. All the tables had white lace doilies under the lamps, and the pictures were all framed in heavy, dark-looking wood. It was nice furniture – I knew that – but it was old and curved, with fat legs. It seemed unusual for a man to live here. It was nothing like we had. Our furniture was not all the same. And the walls in our house were painted and did not have wallpaper.

Warren Miller limped through the living room back into the kitchen where he was cooking, but right away brought my mother a big drink of what he was drinking, which must've been gin. My mother stood over the floor furnace for a minute or two, holding her drink, then she smiled at me and began to walk around the house looking at pictures on top of the piano, and picking up and examining whatever was on the tables, while I sat on the stiff, wool-covered couch and did nothing but wait. Warren Miller had told us he was cooking Italian chicken, and I was ready to eat it.

Walking around Warren Miller's house my mother looked pretty in her green dress and green shoes. I remember that very well. She had gotten warm standing over the furnace, and her face was pink. She was smiling as she looked around, touching things as if she liked everything that was there.

'So,' Warren Miller called out from the kitchen, 'how's your old man doing, Joe?' He was talking loud, and we couldn't see him, though we could hear him cooking, rattling pans and making noises. I wished I could've seen inside the kitchen, but I couldn't.

'He's doing fine,' I said.

'Joe just talked to him on the telephone,' my mother said loudly.

69

'Did he say it was a tragedy out there? That's what they usually say. Everything's a tragedy when they can't put it out.'

'No,' she said. 'He didn't say it was.'

'Did he say he was coming home soon?' Warren Miller said.

'No,' I said. 'He didn't mention that.' On the table beside me was a cold cigar butt in an ashtray, and under it the book my mother had lent to him.

'Women are fighting this fire,' my mother said. 'I read that in the paper.' She was standing, holding a framed photograph of a smiling woman with a dark upper lip. She had picked it up off the piano.

'Women are better at it than men,' Warren Miller said. He appeared limping out of the kitchen door, holding three stacked plates with silverware on top of them. He still had the towel stuffed in his pants. 'They know what you're supposed to run from.'

'You can't run away from everything,' my mother said, and she turned the frame so Warren could see it as he put the plates down on the dining table, which had an expensive-looking white tablecloth over it and was on one side of the living room. 'Who's this pictured?' my mother said.

'That's my wife,' Warren said. 'Formerly. She knew when to run.'

'I'm sure she regrets it, too.' My mother put the picture back down where it had been, and took a drink of her drink.

'She hasn't decided to call up to say so yet. But maybe she will. I'm not dead yet,' Warren said. He looked at my mother and smiled the way he'd smiled at me out on the front steps, as if something wasn't funny.

'Life, life, life, life,' my mother said. 'Life's long.' She suddenly walked across to where Warren Miller was standing beside the dining room table, put her hands on his cheeks, still holding her glass, and kissed him right on the mouth. 'You poor old thing,' she said. 'Nobody's nice enough to you.' She took another big drink of her gin, then

70

looked at me on the couch. 'You don't mind it if I give Mr Miller an innocent kiss, do you, Joe?' she said. She was drunk and she wasn't acting the way she ordinarily would. She looked at Warren Miller again. He had a red smear of her lipstick on his mouth. 'Is something waiting to begin or has it already happened?' she said, because neither of us had said anything. We hadn't moved.

'Everything's in front of us,' Warren Miller said. He looked at me and grinned. 'I've got a big dago dinner cooked up in there,' he said, starting to limp toward the kitchen. 'We have to get this boy fed, Jeanette, or he won't be happy.'

'Not that he's happy now,' my mother said, holding her empty glass. She looked at me again and touched both corners of her mouth with her tongue, then walked straight to the front window of the house where you could see out toward town, and toward our house, empty back on Eighth Street. I don't know what she thought I was thinking. Dislike or surprise or shock at her, I would guess – for bringing me here or for being here herself, or for kissing Warren Miller in front of me, or for being drunk. But I was only aware at that moment that things felt out of control and I did not know how to bring them back, sitting in Warren Miller's living room. We would need to go home to do that. And I guessed she was looking out at the dark toward our house because she wanted to be there. I was relieved, though, that my father didn't know about all this because he wouldn't have understood it even as well as I did. And I told myself, sitting there, that if I ever had the opportunity to tell him about all this, I wouldn't do it. I would never do it as long as I lived, because I loved them.

In a little while Warren Miller brought out a big red bowl of what he called chicken cacciatore and a jug of wine in a basket, and we all three sat down at the table with the white tablecloth and ate. My mother was in an odd mood at first, but she became better, and as she ate she began to find her good spirits again. Warren Miller ate with his napkin tucked into his shirt collar, and my mother said that was the old-fashioned way to eat, and he must've learned it in the old West, but that she didn't want to see me eating that way. Though after a while we all put our napkins in our collars and laughed about it. Nobody talked about the fire. Once Warren Miller looked across the table at me and told me he thought my father had a strong character, and that he fought the circumstances, and that he was a man somebody would be lucky to have working for him, and that when my father came back from the fire he – Warren – would find a job for him, one that had a bright future to it. He said a smart man could make money in the car business, and he and my father would discuss that when the time came.

My mother didn't talk much, though she was having a good time, I thought. She was affected by Warren Miller, by something in him she liked, and she did not mind me seeing it. She smiled and leaned on the table and talked some about Boise, Idaho, where there was a hotel she liked with a good restaurant in it, and about Grand Coulee where she had been fishing with her father when she was a little girl, and where Warren Miller had been. She talked about once seeing the Great Salt Lake from the air, and what that was like, and about Lewiston. She said it was never cold there because of the special climate, and that she wasn't looking forward to the winter coming in Great Falls, because the wind blew for weeks at a time and that after a while, she knew, constant wind would make you crazy. She did not mention the Helen Apartments or about teaching at the air base, or even about working at the grain elevator. All that seemed to have gone away, as if it was a dream she'd had, and the only real worlds were back in Idaho where she'd been happy, and in Warren Miller's house where she was happy to be at that moment.

She asked Warren Miller how he had made his money, and whether he had gone to college to start, because she wanted me to go to college. And Warren, who had lit a big black cigar by then and taken his napkin out of his collar, sat back in his chair and said he had gone to Dartmouth College in the East, and had majored in history because his father had been a college professor of that in Bozeman and insisted, but that Montana was not a place where an education made any difference to anything. He'd learned everything that meant anything, he said, in the Army, in Burma in World War II, where he had been a major in the Signal Corps and where nobody knew how to do anything right.

'Other people's incompetency is what makes you rich,' he said, and tapped the ash off his cigar into an ashtray. 'Money begets money based on no other principle. It almost doesn't matter what you do. I came back from Korea and I was a farmer, and then I got into the oil leasing business and went to Morocco with that, and then I came back here and bought those elevators and the car agency and the crop insurance business. I'm not very smart. Plenty of people are smarter than I am. I'm just progressive.' Warren pushed his big hands back through his glistening hair and smiled across the table at my mother. 'I'm fifty-five years young, but I'm that smart.'

'You're young for your age, though,' my mother said, and smiled back at him. 'You should probably write your personal memoirs someday.' Warren Miller and my mother looked at each other from across the table and I thought they knew something I didn't know.

'Why don't we listen to some music,' Warren Miller said suddenly. 'I bought a record today.'

My mother looked around then at the brightly lit room behind her. 'I'd like to know where the restroom is.' She smiled at me. 'Do you know where it is, Joe?'

'Go through the bedroom, Jenny,' Warren Miller said. 'All the lights are turned on.'

73

I had never heard anyone call her that before, and I must've looked at my mother in a way to let her know I thought there was something surprising about it.

'Oh, for goodness' sake, Joe, accuse me of something that matters,' she said. She got up, and I could tell she had drunk too much because she kept her hand on the back rail of the chair and looked from me to Warren and back again, still standing, her eyes shining in the light. 'Put some music on now,' she said. 'Some people might care to dance after while.'

'We will,' Warren Miller said. 'That's a good idea. When you come back we will.' But he sat still in his chair, holding his cigar over the ashtray. My mother looked at both of us again as if she couldn't see us clearly, then walked into the bedroom and closed the door behind her.

Warren Miller took a long puff on his cigar and blew the smoke up into the room, then held his cigar half onto the ashtray again. The big gold ring he had on his finger, the one I'd felt yesterday, had a square red stone on the top of it and a white diamond stone in the middle of that. It looked like a thing you would never forget you had on.

'I own an airplane,' Warren Miller said to me. 'Have you ever been up in one of those?'

'No,' I said, 'I haven't.'

'You get a different perspective when you're up there like that,' he said. 'The whole world's different. Your town becomes just a little bitty town. I'll take you up with me, and let you handle the controls. Would you like to do that?'

'I'd like to go sometime,' I said.

'You can fly to Spokane and eat lunch and come back. We can take your mother. Would you like that?'

'I don't know,' I said. But I thought she would like it.

'And are you going to go to college like she says,' Warren Miller asked me.

'Yes,' I said. 'I hope so.'

'Where?' he said. 'Which one are you aiming at?'

74

'Harvard,' I said. And I wished I knew where Harvard was, and that I had a reason for saying I wanted to go there.

'It's a good one,' Warren Miller said. He reached up and took the jug of red wine in one hand and poured some into his glass. 'Once,' he said, and he put the jug down, and he sat a second without saying anything. His hair was gleaming in the light, and he blinked his eyes several times behind his glasses. 'Once, when I was flying, it was in the fall, like it is now. Only colder, and it wasn't this dry. I was flying up to look at some poor man's hailed-on wheat crop where I held a policy. And I could see all these geese flying down from Canada. They were all in their formations, you know. Big V's.' He drank half his glass of wine in one gulp and licked his lips. 'I was up there among them. And do you know what I did?' He looked at me and put his cigar back in his mouth and crossed his legs so I could see his brown cowboy boots, which were shiny and without any fancy design on them like other boots I'd seen men wear in Montana.

'No,' I said, though I thought it would be something I wouldn't believe, or something impossible, or that no one would do. He was drunk, too, I thought.

'I opened back my window,' he said, 'and I turned off the engine.' Warren Miller stared at me. 'Four thousand feet up. And I just listened. They were all right up there around me. And they were honking and honking, way up in the sky where no one ever heard them before except God himself. And I thought to myself, this is like seeing an angel. It's a great privilege. It was the most wonderful thing I ever did in my life. Ever will do.'

'Were you afraid?' I said, because all I could think of was what I would've felt and what an airplane would do if its engine was turned off, and how long you could stay up in the air without crashing.

'I was,' Warren Miller said. 'I was afraid. I certainly was. Because I didn't think about anything. I was just up there. I could've been one of those geese, just for that minute. I'd lost all humanity, and I had all these people trusting me on the ground. I had my wife and my mother and four businesses. It wasn't that I didn't care about them. I just didn't even think about them. And then when I did, that's when it scared me. Do you understand what I'm talking about, Joe?'

'Yes,' I said, though I didn't. I only understood that it meant a great deal to Warren Miller and was supposed to mean something to me.

He sat back in his chair. He had leaned forward when he was telling me about hearing the geese. He picked up his wine glass and drank the rest of what was in it. Far away, behind walls, I could hear water running in pipes. 'Do you want a glass of wine?' Warren Miller said.

'Okay,' I said.

He poured some wine for me and more for himself. 'Here's to the angels,' he said, 'and to your old man not getting burned up like a piece of bacon.'

'Thank you,' I said for some reason.

He pushed his wine glass toward mine, but they never actually touched before he pulled back and drank half of his again. I took a small drink of mine and I hated the taste, which seemed both sweet and vinegary at the same time, and I put my glass back down. And I felt, just for a moment, with the lights all on and Warren Miller in front of me, breathing a heavy breath that I could smell and that was like the wine and whatever Warren Miller himself smelled like, that I was in a dream, one that would go on and on, and maybe I would never wake up out of it. My life had suddenly become *this*, which wasn't awful but wasn't the way it had been. My mother was out of sight, I was alone, and in that brief instant I missed my father more than I ever missed him again or had before. I know I almost broke down and cried for all the things I didn't have then and was afraid I wouldn't have again.

'Your mother has a nice frame,' Warren Miller said. He held his glass in one hand and he touched his cold cigar with the other. He seemed very big to me. 'I admire her very much. She puts herself forward nicely in the world.'

'I think so, too,' I said.

'That's what *you* should do.' Warren Miller made a fist with his right hand and held it up so that his big gold ring with the red-ruby stone faced out at me. 'What do you think this is?' he said.

'I don't know,' I said.

He pushed the fist closer to me then. 'It's the Scottish Rite,' he said. 'I'm a Thirty-third Degree Mason.' His fist was wide and thick and packed-looking. It looked like a fist that had not ever hit anything, because everything would get out of its way if it could. 'You can touch it,' he said.

I put my finger on the ring, onto the smoothed red stone and then on the diamond that was embedded in it. On the gold were tiny carvings I couldn't make out.

'It's the all-seeing eye,' Warren Miller said, and kept his fist out as if he had detached it from his body. 'Is your father a Mason?'

'No,' I said, though I didn't know if he was or not. I didn't know what Warren Miller was talking about, but I thought it was because he was drunk.

'You aren't Catholic, are you?' he said.

'No,' I said. 'We don't go to a church.'

'That doesn't matter,' he said, peering at me from behind his glasses. 'You should be in touch with a group of boys your own age. Would you like to do that? I'd be happy to arrange it.'

'That would be fine.' I heard a door open and close, heard more water running in the pipes.

'Boys need a start into life,' Warren Miller said. 'It's not always easy. Luck plays a part in it.'

'Do you have any children,' I asked.

He looked at me strangely. He must've believed I was thinking about what he'd been saying, but I wasn't.

'No,' he said. 'I never did. I don't much like them.'

'Why not?' I said.

'I never knew any, I guess,' he said.

'Where is your wife now,' I asked. But he didn't answer me because my mother opened the bedroom door, and he looked up at her and smiled as if she was the most important person in the world.

'The pretty lady's back,' Warren Miller said. And he got up and went limping across the room away from me and toward the hi-fi set sitting on top of a big chest of drawers against the wall. I had not even noticed it, but it stood out from everything else once you saw it. 'I forgot all about the music,' he said. He opened one of the drawers and took out a record, still in its sleeve-case. 'We'll play something good,' he said.

'You keep everything very neat in here,' my mother said. 'You don't need another wife. You're enough of one yourself.' She put both her palms to her face then and patted her cheeks as if she had washed her face in the bathroom and it was still damp. I had seen her do that before. She was looking around as if the room looked different to her now. Her voice sounded different. It sounded deeper, as if she was catching a cold or had just waked up. 'It's such a pretty little house, too,' my mother said. She looked at me and smiled and hugged her arms.

'I'll die in it one of these days,' Warren Miller said as he was bent over reading the record label.

'That's a happy thought,' my mother said, and shook her head. 'Maybe we should dance before that happens. If you're already thinking that way.'

Warren Miller looked at my mother, and his glasses caught the reflection of the ceiling light. 'We'll dance,' he said.

'Is Warren going to get you into Dartmouth or whatever it is?' my mother said to me. She was standing in the middle of the room, her lips pushed out some as if she was trying to decide something.

'We haven't discussed that subject,' Warren Miller said. 'I was getting him interested in the DeMolay.'

'Oh, that,' my mother said. 'That's just a lot of hooey, Joe. My father was in that. Warren needs to get you into Dartmouth. That's better than Harvard, I've heard. Anybody can get in DeMolay. It's like the Elks.'

'It's better,' Warren said. 'Catholics and Jews aren't in. Not that I care about them.'

'Are you a Democrat?' my mother said.

'When they run anybody good,' Warren Miller said, 'which is not the case now.' He put the record down onto the hi-fi table.

'My family favors the working man,' my mother said. She picked up my glass of wine and took a drink of it.

'Well, you should think that over again,' Warren said, and then he set the needle arm down onto the record, and there was a lot of music all at once in the little living room.

My mother put the wine glass back on the table and started to dance all by herself then, her arms in the air and a look on her face that seemed like a determined look. 'Cha-cha-cha-cha,' is what she said, because it was that type of music, music you could get on the radio from Denver late at night and that I knew she listened to, music with drums and a trumpet and a whole band in the background.

'Do you like this?' Warren Miller said over the music. He was standing there smiling while my mother danced by herself.

'I certainly do,' she said, and she was snapping her fingers and saying 'cha-cha-cha', in time to the music. She grabbed my hands where I was sitting. 'Come on, Joe, and dance with your mother,' she said, and she tried to pull me out of the chair and up onto my feet. I remember her hands were very cold and felt small and thin. I stood up, though I certainly did not want to and couldn't dance at all. My mother pulled me and pushed me back away, and said 'cha-cha-cha', and looked down at my feet, which were moving in

79

confused ways, stepping up and back. Her arms were stiff, and mine were stiff too. It was a terrible thing to do – and to have to do – with your mother, in a strange house, in front of a man I didn't know and didn't like.

When I had stepped forward and back at least ten times I just quit altogether, and let my arms go rubber and stood still, so that my mother just stopped herself and looked at me with disgust.

'You're a terrible dancer, Joe,' she said to me over the music. 'You have anvils for feet. I'm ashamed of you.' She let go of my hands and just stared up at the low ceiling, right into the light globe as if she hoped something or somebody would appear in my place when she looked back.

'You have to dance with me, Warren,' she said. 'My son won't dance with me, and there's nobody else here.' She turned around to Warren Miller and held out her bare arms toward him. 'Come on, Warren,' she said, 'Joe wants me to dance with you. You're the host. You have to do what the guests want. No matter how silly it is.'

'I'll try. All right,' Warren Miller said. He came toward my mother, across the room. His big limp made him look like a man who could never dance and would never want to. He walked, in fact, as if he had a wooden leg.

My mother started dancing by herself again before he even started to try. She was saying 'cha-cha-cha', and when Warren Miller got in her arms' reach, she took his big hands and started to push him backward and then pull him forward the way she'd done with me. And Warren Miller kept up. Every time he moved backward, he went down into his limp, and it looked like he was going to fall, but then my mother would pull his arms hard and he looked ready to stumble forward into her. My mother kept saying, 'cha-cha, cha-cha-cha', with the music, and going forward and back on her toes, and telling Warren not to watch his feet but just to move the way she did, and Warren was limping and ducking his head, but staying up, and after a few times, he was on his toes, too, and seemed light on his feet somehow, the way a big animal can move. He had a smile on his face, and he began to say 'cha-cha-cha' with my mother, and to look at her face and not at his feet, which were scuffing the floor in his boots. My mother let go of his hands after a minute and put hers on his shoulders, and he put his hands on her waist, and they danced like that, then, together – my mother on her toes and Warren with his limp.

'Look at this, Joe,' my mother said. 'Isn't this wonderful? My God, Warren's a man who can dance. He's one in a million.' She threw her head back and let hair hang off her shoulders while she kept on dancing, letting her head sway from side to side with the drumbeats. And it seemed to me she probably did not want me to watch her. I felt, in fact, like I was doing something I shouldn't be doing, so I got up and walked into the bedroom where my mother had gone, and closed the door.

Through the wall the music made a sound as if something was hitting the floor. I could hear their feet shuffling, and both of them laughing as if they were having a wonderful time.

I had nothing to do in the bedroom. All the lights were on. The windowpanes were shiny and through them I could see into the house next door. An old man and an older woman – older than Warren – were sitting side by side in chairs watching a television in the dark. I couldn't see the screen, but both the man and the woman were laughing. I knew they could see me if they looked around, and maybe they could even feel me watching them, and would think I was a burglar and be afraid if they saw me, so that I stepped away from the window.

It was Warren Miller's bedroom. The walls were pale blue and there was a large bed with a white cover and a curved headboard, and a matching bureau with a TV set on top. A lamp with a yellow globe, like the one in the front window, was on the bed table. A fat wallet and some change were on top of the bureau, beside a folded piece of paper that had my mother's name and telephone number written on it. My father's name was underlined below that, and below it was my own name–Joe–with a check beside it. There was nothing wrong with that, I thought. My mother worked for Warren Miller now. He wanted to give my father a job in the future and put me in the DeMolay club.

I walked into the bathroom, where the light was off. I knew my mother had turned it off, and I turned it on again. Over the music in the living room I heard my mother say out loud, 'It's passionate music, isn't it?' And then their feet scuffed on the floor some more.

The bathroom was all white with white towels and a white tub. I could see where my mother had dried her hands on a towel. I could see hairs that were hers on the white sink top, could smell her perfume in the warm air. Warren's possessions were laid out in a straight row: a safety razor, a tube of shaving cream, a bottle of red hair tonic, a leather bottle of shaving lotion, a pair of silver tweezers, a long black comb and a brush with yellow bristles that had a strap across the top of it and the initials WBM on the leather. I was not looking for anything. I only wanted to be out of the living room where the music was going and Warren Miller and my mother were dancing. I opened the drawer under the sink and only a white washrag was there, folded and clean with a new bar of soap on top.

I closed the drawer and walked back into the bedroom and opened the closet. Warren's suits were hanging in a row there and several large pairs of shoes–one a pair of brown golf shoes–were lined up under them. An Army uniform was hung at the end, and on the floor inside the door was a pair of women's silver high heels.

Behind the suits on the closet wall were pictures and

other things hung in frames. I pulled the light string and pushed the suits apart to see. It smelled like mothballs, and it was cool. Warren Miller's discharge certificate from the Army and his graduation diploma from Dartmouth College were hanging side by side. There was a picture of two men in uniforms standing beside an old airplane at the edge of what looked like a jungle. There was also a framed picture of Warren Miller standing beside the woman whose picture was in the living room. They were both dressed in nice clothes, and the woman was smiling and holding some white flowers. They were squinting in the sun. The picture had been taken years before, but Warren looked familiar, big and heavy and tall, only with thicker, shorter hair. To the side of the pictures was a metal leg brace hung from a nail, a shiny steel device with pink straps and movable buckles and hinges that must've been what Warren wore on his leg, and that made him limp but also able to walk at all.

I closed the closet and walked back into the bedroom, which seemed warmer. A book was face-down on the lighted bed table. The cover had a painting of a cowboy riding a galloping white horse, holding a woman whose blouse was torn, and shooting at men who were chasing them on horses. *Texas Trouble* was the title.

I opened the bed table drawer and inside were some golf tees and a small worn Bible with a green bookmark in it. The drawer smelled like talcum powder. Two silver knives like the one he had given me, with BURMA-1943 engraved on them, were also in the drawer. And there was a gun, a small automatic with a short barrel and a black plastic handle. I had picked up guns before. My father kept one in the same place Warren Miller did. This one was a small calibre—a .32 or even less than that, something to scare people with or wound them but not necessarily kill them. I picked it up and it was heavier than I thought it would be, and seemed more dangerous than I'd thought at first. I took a good grip, put my finger around the trigger, pointed the gun at the closet door, and made a soft little popping sound with my lips. I thought about shooting someone, following them, aiming, holding my arm and hand steady, then pulling the trigger. I had no one in mind to shoot. Shooting someone was a thing I was sure I'd never do. There *were* those things, after all. And it was all right to know about them long before you had the opportunity or the desire.

I turned to put the gun back in the drawer, but I saw that there was a white handkerchief that had been lying underneath it. The handkerchief had the same initials that were on the brush–WBM–stitched on the corner in blue letters. And for some reason I pressed my hand on the handkerchief, which was folded into a square. And I felt something inside or underneath it. I turned the handkerchief back so I could see what I'd felt, and there was one prophylactic rubber in a red and gold tinfoil envelope. I had seen one before. In fact, I'd seen them plenty of times, though I had never used one. Boys at the school I'd gone to in Lewiston had them and showed them off. No one I knew in school in Great Falls had shown me one, though the boys talked about fucking girls there, and I believed they had them and knew about them. I had never known my father to have any, although I had thought about his having them, and had even looked for them in his drawers. I don't know what I would've done if I'd found them, because what I thought about the subject was that it was his business, his and my mother's. I wasn't innocent about life, about what people did with each other when they were alone. I knew they did what they pleased.

It did not surprise me that Warren Miller had a rubber, though I could not think about him using it. When I tried I could only picture him sitting on the side of the bed where I was, wearing his underwear, holding the edge of the mattress, wearing socks and staring at nothing but the floor. A woman was not involved. But I thought it was his right to have a rubber if he wanted it. I picked it up off the white handkerchief. Murphy was the name of the company that made it, in Akron, Ohio. I squeezed the envelope between my fingers, felt the outline of it inside. I smelled it, and it smelled starchy from the handkerchief. I thought about the possibility of opening it. But I had nothing whatsoever that I could do with it.

I laid it back between the folds of the handkerchief and put the gun back on top. Though as I did that I thought about Warren's wife, Marie LaRose or whatever her name was, and that she had gone out of this house, this very room, and didn't intend to come back. And that Warren was alone here, with that to remember and think about. I closed the drawer, then walked back out to where Warren Miller and my mother were, where the music had stopped.

My mother was sitting on the piano bench, her legs pushed out in front of her. Her green shoes weren't off, but her green dress was up above her knees and she was fanning herself with a sheet of music off the piano. She smiled at me as if she'd expected to see me come out of the room at that very moment. Warren Miller was sitting at the dinner table, where all the dishes and plates were. He was smoking his cigar again.

'Did you look into all of Warren's drawers in there?' my mother said, smiling and fanning herself. Her voice was still deep. 'You'll find out his secrets. I'm sure he has a lot of them.'

'None that I wouldn't share with him,' Warren said. He had unbuttoned his top shirt button and was sweating under his arms.

'When Joe's father and I first married,' my mother said, 'I rented a sailor costume and did a little cute tap dance when he got home from teaching golf. It was an anniversary present. He loved it. Something made me think of that just now.'

'I bet he did. I bet that was nice.' Warren took his glasses off and wiped them with his napkin, then dabbed his eyes with it. His face looked larger without his glasses and whiter. 'Your mother's a very passionate dancer, you know that, Joe?'

'He means I'll go till I drop,' my mother said. 'It's hot as fire in this house, of course. Anybody'd drop dead.' My mother looked at me as if she'd just noticed me for the first time since I came back into the room. 'What would you like to do now, sweetheart?' she said. 'I'm sure we're just boring you to death. At least I'm sure *I* am.'

'No,' I said. 'You're not. I'm not bored.'

'Do you know how Warren injured his leg,' my mother asked. She pulled a strand of damp hair away from her forehead and fanned her face some more.

'No,' I said, and I sat down where I'd been sitting at the dinner table, beside Warren Miller.

'Well, would you care to?' she said.

'I guess so,' I said.

'Well. He was hit from behind by a big roll of barbed wire when he was wading across the Smith River up to his rear end. Isn't that right, Warren? It was underwater, and you didn't see it coming. Is that what you said?'

'That's right,' Warren Miller said. He looked a little uncomfortable at my mother's telling this.

'And the lesson is what?' My mother smiled. 'Warren seems to think we need to learn a lesson from everything. The world should keep it in mind.'

'Something's always up there that can take you away,' Warren Miller said, seated at the dinner table, his big legs crossed in front of him.

'Or not,' my mother said.

'Or not – that's right, too,' Warren said, and smiled at my mother. He liked her. I could tell that was true.

'Joe and I have to go home now, Warren,' my mother said, and she stood up. 'I'm irritable all of a sudden and Joe's bored.'

'I had hopes you'd stay all night,' Warren Miller said, his

hands on his knees, smiling. 'It's gotten colder. And you're drunk.'

'I *am* drunk,' my mother said. She looked at the old piano behind her, and set the music down on the little stand. 'That's not a crime yet, is it?' She looked at me. 'Did you know Warren could play the piano, sweetheart? He's very talented. You should be like him.'

'There's another bedroom,' Warren Miller said, and pointed to the other room, where the light was on and the foot of another bed was visible.

'I never intended to stay here all night,' my mother said. She looked around the little living room as if she was looking for a coat to wear outside. 'Joe's a very good driver. His father taught him.'

'You have to put something on,' Warren Miller said. He stood up and went limping off into the other bedroom, the one I hadn't been in.

'Warren's going to give me one of his wife's wraps, I believe,' my mother said, and looked annoyed. 'You don't mind driving, do you? I'm sorry. I am drunk.'

'It's all right,' I said. 'I don't mind.'

'Combat experience,' my mother said. 'That's what my mother used to call it when my father would get drunk and roar in and start making demands. You'll get a big promotion someday. Which is to say, you'll be grown up and can leave.'

Warren Miller limped back into the room, holding a man's brown coat. 'This'll do a good job,' he said. He came and held the coat while my mother put it on. She buttoned all three buttons, and when she did she looked like someone else – not a man, but like somebody I didn't know.

'Don't you have one of your mother's coats?' my mother said.

'I gave them away to the poor,' Warren said.

'Did you give your wife's away, too?' She smiled at him.

'Maybe I'll just throw them away,' he said.

'Don't do that,' my mother said. 'She might be waiting upstream. You never know.'

'I hope not,' Warren said. And suddenly he took my mother's shoulders, pulled her to him and kissed her on the mouth right in front of me. And I did not like that. My mother pulled away as if she hadn't liked it either. She started toward the front door.

'Come on, the fun's over here, Joe,' she said.

I followed her, though I glanced at Warren Miller, and he had a look on his face I didn't like. He was angry, and I could see him breathing under his white shirt. He looked like somebody who could hurt you and who *would* if he lost his temper or had a reason. I didn't like him, and in fact I never liked him again. What I wanted to do was get away from him, get out into the night with my mother, and go home.

It was cold in the car when we got inside. I sat behind the wheel and put my hands on it, waiting for my mother to find the keys, which were on the seat. The wheel was cold and hard to move. Down the street the blue light at the Italian place was still shining like a haze.

'My heart's just pounding away,' my mother said. 'Switch on the light in here.' I turned on the inside light and she bent over looking for the keys and finally found them in the crack of the seat. 'I drank too much,' she said. 'That makes your heart race.' She handed me the keys. Then she said, 'Stay here, Joe. I don't want to wear this coat home.'

She opened the door, got out, and went back across the street and up the concrete steps to where the lights were still on in the window. I watched while she rang the bell, then waited. Warren Miller came to the door and she stepped inside already taking the coat off. I saw them walk past the window. He had hold of her arm, and they were talking. Then I couldn't see them anymore.

I sat there in the cold car with the lights turned off and waited, watching down the street. I watched as a group of men came outside the Italian restaurant and walked into the empty street. They stood and talked to each other with their hands in their pockets, then one of the men hit another one in the arm as a joke, and then they all left in different directions. Car lights went on at the curb farther down the street, then the cars drove away. I sat still as one passed by me. In a minute a man and a woman came out together, dressed in heavy winter coats. They walked out into the street the way the others had, and stood talking. Then the man walked with the woman to a car and opened the door. He kissed her, then she got inside and started the engine and drove away. The man found his car farther down the street and drove away, too, in the opposite direction.

I looked up at Warren Miller's house and tried to guess how long I'd waited and how long I would have to wait, and what my mother was saying about the coat and not wearing it. I didn't see how it mattered, and what I believed she was saying to him was that she didn't like being kissed, and especially not like that, in front of me, and that she would not stand for it again. I wondered what Warren Miller did with his boat, which I could see in the driveway nosed up, wondered what body of water he put it in and if I would ever get to go in it, or in his airplane – to Spokane – or if I would ever see him again. And for some reason it seemed to me that I wouldn't, and for that reason I wished I'd put the silver knife he'd given me back in the drawer with the other two. I had no use for it now and I thought I would throw it away when I had the chance, throw it in the river when we drove back across on the way home. And something about that thought, about Warren Miller and the way he looked the last time I'd seen him, through the window of his house, with my mother in the living room, made me remember him – a large smiling man my father had taught to play golf, someone whose name I hadn't remembered or hadn't said anything to, only saw, maybe through a window or inside a car, or at a distance hitting a golf ball. I had only that part of a memory.

I wondered if there was some pattern or an order to things in your life – not one you knew but that worked on you and made events when they happened seem correct, or made you confident about them or willing to accept them even if they seemed like wrong things. Or was everything just happening all the time, in a whirl without anything to stop it or cause it – the way we think of ants, or molecules under the microscope, or the way others would think of us, not knowing our difficulties, watching us from another planet?

From down the hill I heard the eleven o'clock shift whistle. Men at the oil refinery were going home, and I was tired and wanted Warren Miller to be out of our life, since he didn't seem to have a place in it.

I got out of the car into the cold street and looked at the house. I thought my mother would come out the door at any minute, but there was no movement there. The porch light was off, but the yellow light inside was still lit. I thought I heard music, boogie-woogie music – a piano and some horns – but I couldn't be sure. It could've been from the Italian place. I waited a minute, just watching the house. I didn't know how much time had gone by since my mother had gone inside. I heard a switch engine in the freight yards down the hill. Several more cars drove past me. Finally I walked across the street and up the steps, then stopped halfway and listened. The music was louder and coming from Warren Miller's living room. I wanted to shout for my mother to come out, or to come to the window and give me a signal. But I didn't want to shout out 'Mother' or 'Jeanette'.

I walked up the front steps onto the porch, and instead of going to the door and knocking, I went to the front window, through which I could see inside the living room. I saw the table with our dishes still on it. I saw the door to the kitchen was open and the doors to both bedrooms, and beyond them the bathroom where I had been and where the light shone on the white tiles. And I saw my mother and Warren Miller. They were standing in the middle of the living room, right where they'd been when they were dancing. And I think I almost did not see them. If I'd gone back to the car then I wouldn't have seen them at all, or would not have remembered it. The coat my mother had been wearing was lying on the floor, and she had her bare arms around Warren Miller's neck and was kissing him and putting her hands in his hair, standing in the middle of the bright room. Warren Miller had pulled my mother's green dress up from behind her so that you could see where her stockings were held by white elastic straps, and you could see her white underpants. And even though he had his cigar in his hand, held between his fingers, he was holding my mother outside her underwear, and pulling her toward him so hard that he picked her up off the floor and held her against him while he kissed her and she kissed him.

I stood at the window and watched what they did—which was no more than I have said—until my mother's feet touched the floor again, and I thought they might stop kissing suddenly and both turn and look at me, where I was perfectly visible through the window glass. I did not even want to stop them, or make them do what they didn't want to do. I just wanted to keep watching until whatever was supposed to happen did happen. Though when my mother's feet touched the floor I moved to the side, and when I was away from the window I could not move back into it again. I was afraid they would see me. And I simply turned around and walked back down the steps and across the street to the car, got in the driver's seat, and waited for my mother to finish what she was doing there and come out so we could go home.

In not very much time the front door of the house opened and my mother walked out, not wearing the coat, just in her green dress. She walked straight down the steps. I didn't see Warren Miller. The door stayed open only for a moment, and then it closed. The porch light did not come on again, though I saw a light go off inside the house.

My mother hurried across the street and got into the car beside me and shivered when she closed the door. 'He needs a nicer house,' she said. She crossed her arms together in front of her and she shivered again and shook her head. I could smell the sweet greasy odor of the red hair tonic that was in Warren Miller's bathroom. 'Aren't you cold?' she said. 'It's getting colder. It'll snow next, and then what?'

'It's not supposed to,' I said. I hadn't started the car yet. We were just sitting in the dark.

'Good,' she said and blew on the back of her hands. 'I surprised myself. I had a good time. Did you have one, too?'

'Yes,' I said. 'I did,' though that was a lie.

'I didn't want that old coat, though. I just didn't.' She put her hands to her face. 'My cheeks are hot.' She turned and looked into the back seat as if she expected to see someone there, then she looked at me in the dark. 'Did you like him?'

'No,' I said. 'Not too much.'

'Are you sorry you came, then? Is that what you're telling me?'

'I don't know,' I said. 'I haven't thought about that.' I touched the key and turned it to start the car. The heater fan came on, blowing cold air.

'Well, think about it,' she said.

'I will.'

'What will you think about me after I'm dead?' she said. 'Maybe you haven't thought about that yet, either.'

'I've thought about that,' I said, and I switched off the heater.

'And? What's my verdict? I can take it if it's guilty.'

'I'd miss you,' I said, 'I know that.'

'Warren says he means it about taking you up in his airplane,' she said. 'He says you can learn all of Morse code in one afternoon's lesson. I always wanted to know that. I could send secret messages to people in other places.'

'Why did his wife leave him,' I asked. It was all I could think of to say.

'I don't know about it,' my mother said. 'He isn't handsome at all. Though of course men have more ways to be handsome. Unlike women. Do you think you're handsome?' When she said this she looked straight at me. We were just sitting in the car, in front of Warren Miller's house, in the dark, talking. 'You look like your dad. Do you think he's handsome?'

'I think he is,' I said.

'I think he is, too,' my mother said. 'I've always thought he was very handsome.' She put the palm of her hand to the cold window glass beside her, then held it against her cheek. 'It's lonely up here, isn't it? Do you think it's lonely?'

'Right now I do,' I said.

'It's not so much a matter of being alone or wanting somebody who's not there, is it? It's being with people who aren't appropriate enough. I think that's right.'

'May-be,' I said.

'And you're with me.' My mother smiled at me. 'I guess I'm not very appropriate. It's too bad. Too bad for me, I mean.'

'I think you're appropriate,' I said. I looked up at Warren Miller's house and saw that all the lights were turned off in the front room. A single light was burning from the side window. He was in his bedroom, and I could think of him bent over at the closet door, taking off his boots, his hand on the blue wallpaper for balance. Maybe, I thought, he was not to blame for kissing my mother and holding her dress up over her hips. Maybe that's all he could do. Maybe no one was to blame for that, or for much of what happened to anyone.

'Why don't we drive away now?' my mother said to me. 'Do you feel all right?'

'I feel fine,' I said.

'I know you drank some wine.'

'I feel all right,' I said. 'How do you feel?'

'Oh, well,' my mother said. 'How do I feel? I'm afraid of becoming somebody else now, I guess. Somebody very new and different. That's probably how the world works. We just don't know it until it happens. "Ha-ha," I guess is what we should say. "Ha-ha." ' She smiled at me again.

Then I drove off down the street away from Warren Miller's house, thinking that the world was becoming different for me, too, and in a hurry. I could feel it, like a buzz all around me, exactly like my father told me the world felt to him when it began to change.

When we walked into the house that night the telephone was ringing. It was eleven-thirty. My mother went straight back into the kitchen and answered it. It was my father calling from the forest fire.

'Yes, Jerry. How are you?' I heard my mother say. I could see her standing at the kitchen table. She was winding the phone cord around her finger and looking at me through the door as she talked to him. She looked taller than she had looked in Warren Miller's house. Her face looked different, more businesslike, less ready to smile. I stood and watched her as if I was going to talk next, although I knew I wasn't going to.

'Well, that's very good, honey,' my mother said. 'It is. I'm relieved to know that.' She nodded, still watching me. I knew she wasn't thinking about me, maybe wouldn't even have known I was the person she was looking at. 'Well, what a thing to see,' she said. 'My God.' She looked around her

94

and found the cup she had been drinking whiskey out of before we'd left earlier that evening, and stood holding it as she talked. 'Well, is it possible to breathe at all?' she said. 'That's what I've wanted to know. That seemed important.'

Then my father talked for a while. I could hear his voice buzzing in the receiver from all the way across the room.

'Uh-huh,' she said. 'Uh-huh.' She was just holding the empty cup. She even turned it up a last time and let the few drops drain into her mouth while she listened. Then she set it down beside her on the table. 'Yes. You reach your limits. I know that. You have to adapt,' she said. 'How can it happen so fast? My God.' My father talked again, and my mother looked out at me and pointed with her finger toward the hallway, and she mouthed the words, 'Go to bed.'

I wasn't going to get to talk to my father that night, though I wished I could've gotten on the line and told him that I missed him, that we both did, and we wished he'd come home tonight. But that was not what my mother wanted, and I did what she said because I didn't want there to be an argument late at night with my father on the phone, and her drunk and in love with another man.

My mother didn't talk to my father much longer. From my room I could hear a word she would say, then she would lower her voice and talk. I didn't hear my name mentioned or Warren Miller's or the air base job she had applied for that day. I heard the words 'spontaneous' and 'lie' and 'private' and 'sweet'. That was all. And in a few minutes I heard the receiver put down, and a cabinet door open and the sound of glass touching glass.

I was already in bed when my mother came in my room. The ceiling light was still on, and I thought she would turn if off for me. She had another glass of whiskey with her. I had never seen her drink so much as she had on that day and that night. She had not been a drinker before.

'Your father says hello to his only son,' she said, and took a drink. 'He said he saw a bear catch on fire. Isn't that something?' I was just listening to her. 'He said it had climbed a tree to get away and the fire exploded in the branches all around it. The poor bear jumped out completely on fire and ran away. That's a thing to remember, isn't it?'

'Did he say he was coming home,' I asked. I was thinking, lying in my bed, that it might be snowing where he was, and that the fire would go out by itself.

'He may stay on a while longer,' my mother said. 'I didn't ask for the vital details. Are you proud of him? Are you coming to that conclusion?'

'Yes. I am,' I said.

'That's fine,' she said. 'He'd like you to be. I wouldn't talk you out of it.'

'Are you proud of him?' I asked.

'Oh,' my mother said. 'Do you remember when we got very close to the fire when we went up there? And you got out and went over to it – I guess I wanted you to experience it. But when you came back, I told you that the whole fire was just a lot of little separate fires? And once in a while they blew up together and destroyed everything?' She stuck her finger in her glass, then put her finger in her mouth. 'Well, I guess I think nothing's that important by itself,' she said softly.

'I believe that,' I said, though I didn't believe she had answered my question about my father.

'It *is* right,' my mother said, and was irritated. 'I know what's right, for God's sake. I've just never thrown myself into anything like that before.' She took a deep breath and let it out in a rush. She stared out my window into the night. 'What would you think if I killed someone – would you be

96

embarrassed?' She looked at me, and I knew she wasn't thinking of killing anyone.

'Yes,' I said. 'I would. I wouldn't like it.'

'Well. All right, then,' my mother said. 'That's out. I have to figure out something else. Something more interesting.'

'Are you proud of Dad,' I asked. 'You didn't answer that.'

'Oh,' she said. 'No. Not much. You shouldn't let that bother you, though – you know, sweetheart? It's not very important who I'm proud of. Myself. I should just want to be proud of myself. That's all. You have to put your trust into something else now.' She smiled at me. 'I was just wondering why I thought I had to take you with me tonight. We do strange things sometimes. I don't know who I was showing to whom. You probably don't even care about it. It's just one thing, not a lot of things.'

'I thought you wanted me to go with you,' I said.

'Well, that's right. You're right.' She smiled at me again and pushed her fingers back through her hair.

'Did Warren tell you his story about seeing the geese from the airplane?'

'Yes,' I said.

'Isn't that a wonderful story?' my mother said. 'It's baloney, of course. He just thinks things up and says them.' She turned the light off. 'It's diverting, though,' she said, and then she said good night and closed the door behind her.

And I lay in bed for just a little time, thinking before I went to sleep that Warren Miller didn't seem like the kind of man to make a story up. He seemed like the kind of man things happened to, the way my mother had said, and who did the wrong things and tried to act as if he didn't by acting better, a man my father might've said had bad character. I wondered what my father had said about me tonight, if he was mad at me, and if I'd done something wrong and was trying to act as if I hadn't. As I slipped down into sleep I thought I could hear my mother dialing the telephone. I waited, and could feel myself alive while the ringing went on and someone answered somewhere – Warren Miller, I thought, no one else. I heard his voice, 'Yes,' he said, 'yes.' Then it was silent and I went to sleep.

At two o'clock that night I came awake. Down the hall, I heard the toilet running, and I could hear someone jiggling the handle to make the running stop. I listened to the noise of the metal on the tank and the water running through the pipes, and I got out of bed and went to the door of my room and stepped out into the dark hall where I could not be seen. And I waited there until the bathroom door opened and the light cast onto the floor and Warren Miller came out, turned back and clicked off the bathroom light, and then walked in the direction of my mother's room. He was naked. In the light I saw his legs and his chest which were covered with hair. I saw his penis, and when he turned I saw the scars on the back of his legs, where the barbed wire had hit him. It looked to me like skin that had been shot with a shotgun. He was wearing his glasses, and as he walked toward my mother's room I saw how he limped, that one leg, his right one, would not straighten and for that reason made him dip to the side and made his other leg, his good one, throw out farther ahead in a way that made the limp be worse. His white body shone in the dark hallway as he went away from me, and I stood in my tee shirt and underpants as he opened the door to my mother's room – where there was no light – and heard her soft voice from inside say, 'Be quiet, now. Just be quiet.' The door closed, then, and I heard her bed squeeze down under his weight. I heard my mother sigh, and I heard Warren Miller cough and clear his throat. I was cold there, my back to the hall closet door. My legs were cold and my feet and hands were. But I didn't want to move from there because I wanted to know what else would go on and felt that something would.

In the room I heard my mother's soft voice and Warren Miller's. I heard the bed squeeze again and make a thumping noise. I heard my mother say, 'Oh, now,' not in an excited way, just in a way to not like something. The bed made more noise, and I knew I'd slept through other noises already, and that when I thought I'd heard my mother calling Warren Miller on the telephone that is what I had heard.

I heard his bare feet on the floor, then, limping and sliding. I heard the closet door open and the sound of a coat hanger skidding over metal. I could hear the sounds of clothes moving, and of breathing, and of a shoe-step on the floor in the bedroom. And then my mother's door opened again, and she and Warren Miller came out together into the hall. He had on the white shirt and trousers he'd been wearing at his house earlier that night, and he was holding his boots. My mother only had on her bathrobe and a pair of shoes I could hear but not see in the darkness. They did not look in my direction; I knew they did not think of me or where I was. They simply walked across the hallway—they were holding hands one behind the other—and into the kitchen and across the floor to the back door. I heard the back door open, and for just a moment I thought my mother was showing him to the back door so he could leave. But then the back door shut quietly, and the screen door shut quietly outside. And the house was silent and empty except for me in the hallway alone and the sound of the water hissing in the tank where Warren had tried to make it stop but been unable to.

I walked to the back door and looked out. In the moonlight I could see nothing but the corner of the old garage at the back of the lot—a garage we did not use—and the shadow of the birch tree on the ground of the side yard. I could not see my mother and Warren Miller. They were gone.

I walked back into my own room and looked out the window toward the street. And I could see Warren Miller then, and my mother. They were on the sidewalk, walking side by side and no longer holding hands. He still had his boots under his arms, and they were hurrying away from the house, almost running, as if they were cold and wanted to get someplace warmer. Together they hurried out into the dark street. They didn't look either way—my mother held her bathrobe up so she could take longer steps. They did not look back or seem to be saying anything to each other. But I could see from the window that they were hurrying toward a car parked by itself across the street. It was Warren Miller's pink car sitting in the shadows and collected leaves, unnoticeable there if you were not expecting to see it.

When they got to the car my mother hurried around to the passenger's side and got in. Warren Miller got in the driver's side and closed the door after him. The red taillight went on immediately. I saw the interior light snap on, saw them both inside—my mother sitting far across the seat against her door and Warren behind the steering wheel. The motor suddenly came alive and white exhaust blew into the air behind the car. I saw my mother's face turn toward Warren Miller, and I thought she said something about the light, because the interior light went off then, and the brake lights went out. But the car did not move. It just sat in the darkness across the street. I stood at my window and watched, waiting for it to drive away, for my mother and Warren Miller to go off toward wherever they were going—to his house, or a motel or another city, or to someplace where I would never see either of them again. But that is not what happened. The Oldsmobile stayed where it was with its motor running and its lights off, and my mother and him inside. I could not see them in the dark, and little by little the window glass became clouded from their being there inside together breathing.

I stayed at my window and watched the car for a few minutes more. And nothing happened, nothing that I could see, though I supposed I knew what was happening. Just the thing you would think, nothing surprising. One car came down Eighth Street and did not slow down or notice. Its headlights passed over the clouded windows and illuminated the engine exhaust. But I couldn't see either my mother or Warren Miller inside. I wondered if they were in danger of suffocating because of the exhaust filtering back into the car. It was a thing you read about. And I decided that they were. But they knew about that and would have to worry about it themselves. If they died where they were and for the reasons they were there, it would be their fault, and I couldn't help them. And after a few minutes of standing at the cold window, watching the car and its exhaust, I closed my curtain and walked back through the house where I was alone.

From my room I walked into the hall and down to the bathroom. Water was still running in the toilet, and I picked up the lid off the tank, stuck my bare arm down into the cold water until I could feel the slick rubber stopper at the bottom. I held it down until the water stopped running, and my arm felt hard and cold. I waited a minute, it must've been, with my hand in the water so that I was sure the stopper would hold, then I dried my arm and replaced the lid, and tried to think what I should do next—if I should get in bed again and go to sleep, or if I should go in the kitchen and read with the light on, or put on my clothes and walk out into the night away from where my mother was in Warren Miller's car, and maybe not come back, or come back in two days, or call from someplace, or never call.

What I did was to go into the kitchen where my mother's bottle of whiskey was still on the countertop in the dark, and got the flashlight from under the sink. I turned the flashlight on and went with it—shining back down the hall—and into my mother's room where the curtains were drawn shut and the bed was tumbled all around, and a pillow and part of the sheet were on the floor. There was an odd smell in the air there – the smell of my mother's perfume and some other smell also that was like hand lotion, and that wasn't sweet but I thought I knew from someplace but couldn't remember where. I shined the light around – at the clock turned toward the wall by the bed, at the closet door, which was open and my mother's clothes pushed out, at her green dress and green shoes and stockings, which were lying on the one chair. There was nothing in particular I wanted to find, or anything I thought would be secret. It was just my mother's room, with her belongings in it, and nothing she was doing now would make anything there be different or special.

There was no sign of my father in the room, I did notice that – as though he had never lived there. His golf bag was gone. The pictures that he had left on the bureau top were gone. The leather box where he kept his cuff links was put away someplace, some drawer, and the books he kept on the golf game and teaching golf were down off the top of the bureau where he'd had them standing and lined up. There was only a framed picture of him on the wall beside the window, almost hidden by the curtain. Maybe my mother had overlooked that. I shined my flashlight on its glass. In the picture my father was wearing a pair of light-colored pants and light-colored shoes and a white short-sleeved shirt. He was standing alone on some golf course, holding a driver, looking down the open fairway and smiling, ready to hit the ball that was at his feet. And he was young in the picture, his face looked young and his hair was short and his arms looked strong. He looked like a man who knew what he was doing. He could hit the ball out of sight any time he got ready, and was just making sure things were the way he wanted them to be. 'That's the way you play this game,' he had said when he showed me the picture the first time, when I was ten or twelve. 'Like you know what you're doing every second. Clear your mind out. You don't have a care in the world. Then everything you hit goes in the hole. It's when you have a lot on your mind, Joe, that you leave everything short. There's no mystery to it.' It was my father's favorite picture of himself, taken when he and my mother were first married and I was not even dreamed up. As I shined my flashlight on that picture then, onto my father's clean smiling face without a care in the world, I was glad he wasn't here now to know about any of this. I was glad he was where he was, and hoped it somehow could be all over and done with before he came home to find everything in his life and my life and my mother's, too, out of all control and out of all sense.

I looked out my mother's window, between the closed curtains, and into the yard. Maybe ten minutes had gone by since I saw her leave in her bathrobe with Warren Miller carrying his boots. There were no lights on in the houses on our street and no cars moving. I could just see the back of Warren Miller's car, see the exhaust still coming out of it. I could hear, I thought, the low rumbles of the motor. I guessed that whatever they'd been doing in my mother's room had all of a sudden been hard to do or had made too much noise, so that the car had seemed like a better place. Out in our little yard the grass was white with frost and moonlight. The weeping birch tree cast a wider, denser shadow toward the street. A magpie stood in the middle of things there, alone. It moved, a hop one way and another, picked into the grass, looked around, then moved again. I put my flashlight flat against the glass and clicked it on and shined a dim light out onto the bird where it stayed still and did not look up or at me, but stared straight ahead – so it seemed to me – at nothing. It did not know I was there. It could not feel the light that was on it, couldn't see anything different occurring. It just sat as though it was waiting for something to start to happen that would give it a reason to move or fly or even look in one direction or the other. It wasn't afraid simply because it knew nothing to be afraid of. I tapped the cold glass with my fingernail – not loud, just enough for the bird to hear. It turned its head so that its red eyes went right up into the light. And it opened its wings once as though it was stretching, then closed them, hopped once toward me, then flew suddenly straight up at the light and the glass and at me, as if it was about to hit the window or break it through. Only it didn't touch anything, but flew up into the dark and out of my sight completely, leaving me there with my heart pounding, and my light shining onto the cold yard at nothing.

I heard a car door close. I switched off my light and stood by the side of the curtain so that I could still see out but not be seen. I did not hear anyone's voice speak, but my mother appeared on the sidewalk then, hurrying the way she had before, her arms folded across her chest, her shoes tapping the concrete. She turned in the driveway and went out of my sight. And when she did, Warren Miller's car moved away slowly in the dark without its lights. I could hear it, its big muffler making a deeper rumbling sound down the quite street. I saw its taillights snap on red, and then it disappeared.

I walked out of my mother's room and back down the hall in the dark to the spot I had been in when she and Warren Miller had left the house fifteen minutes before, or maybe thirty minutes before. I had lost track of time, though with all of what was going on it didn't seem to matter. I heard my mother open the back door. She opened it just the way she would any day – as if everything was normal. I heard her in the kitchen. The ceiling light went on. I heard her running water in the sink, filling a glass, and I knew she was standing, drinking water in her bathrobe – something anyone would do on any night. I heard her run more water, then wait, then put the glass away and go and lock the door.

Then she walked straight out through the kitchen into the hall where I was waiting in the shadows as I had been before.

But she did not see me. She did not even look in the direction I was, toward my door. She passed across the hall and went into the bathroom. I had only a moment to see her. Her bathrobe was open and I could see her bare knees as she took her steps. Inside, she turned on the light but did not close the door. I could hear her use the toilet and then the flushing sound and water running in the sink and the sound of her washing her hands. I was waiting there, outside the light. I had nothing planned to say or to do. I must've believed I would say something when she came back out, or just wanted to say, 'Hello,' or 'This is all right … I don't mind.' Or 'What are you doing?' But none of those words were in my mind. I was simply there, and it occurred to me that she didn't know it yet. She did not know what I knew about this—about Warren Miller and her, about what I'd seen or thought of it. And until she knew it, until we talked about it—even if she assumed everything and I did, too—it had not exactly happened, and we did not exactly have to have it between us after tonight. It would just be a thing we could ignore and finally forget. And what I should do was go back inside my room, get into my bed and go to sleep, and when I woke up try to think about something else.

But my mother came out of the bathroom before I could move. Again she did not look in my direction. She turned toward her bedroom, where I had been five minutes before. But all at once she turned back because she'd left the light on in the bathroom, and I suppose wanted to turn it off. And that is when she saw me, standing in the shadows in my underwear, watching her like a burglar who'd broken in the house to steal something and been caught.

'Oh God damn it,' my mother said before I could say a word or even move. She came down the hall to where I was, and she slapped me in the face with her open hand. And then she slapped me again with her other hand. 'I'm mad at you,' she said.

'I didn't mean it,' I said. 'I'm sorry.' I didn't try to move or raise my hand or do anything. Her bathrobe was open in front, and she was naked underneath. I could see her stomach and all of that. I had seen my mother naked before but this was different and I wished that she had her clothes on.

'I wish I was dead,' she said, and she turned around and walked back down the hall to her room. She was not crying. And she did not try to close the front of her bathrobe. When she got into the light that came out of the bathroom, she turned around and looked at me. Her face was angry. Her mouth seemed large and her eyes wide open. Her hands were made into fists, and I thought she might be thinking of coming back down the hall and hitting me again. Nothing seemed impossible. 'You probably want to leave, don't you? Now, anyway,' she said. 'Go ahead. That's the way everything always happens. People do things. There isn't any plan. What's next? Who knows?' She raised her hands with her palms up in a way I'd seen people do before. 'If you've got a plan for me, tell me. I'll try to do it. Maybe it'll be better than this.'

'I don't have one,' I said. My face was beginning to throb where she'd hit me. It hadn't hurt at first, but now it did. I wondered if the second time she hadn't hit me with her fist—maybe by accident—because my eye hurt. 'I don't care,' I said. I stood back against the wall and didn't say anything else. I could feel myself breathe, feel my heart beat, feel my hands going cold. I must've been afraid but didn't know it.

'A man like him can be handsome,' my mother said. 'You don't know about that. You don't know anything but just this. I guess I should be more discreet. This house is too small.' She turned around and walked down the hall and into her room. She did not turn the light on. I heard her shoes hit the floor, heard her bed squeeze down as she got into it, and the sound of her bedspread being moved to cover her up. She was going to sleep now. She must've thought that was all there was to do. Neither of us had a plan. 'Your father wants to make things better,' I heard her say out of the dark. 'Maybe I'm not up to that. You can tell him all about this. What's the difference?'

I wanted to say something back, even if she wasn't talking to me but was just talking to herself or no one. I didn't think I would tell my father about this, and I wanted to say so. But I didn't want to be the last one to talk. Because if I spoke anything at all, my mother would stay quiet as if she hadn't heard me, and I would have my own words – whatever they were – to live with, maybe forever. And †here are words, significant words, you do not want to say, words that account for busted-up lives, words that try to fix something ruined that shouldn't be ruined and no one wanted ruined, and that words can't fix anyway. Telling my father about all I'd seen or telling my mother that she could rely on me to say nothing, were those kind of words – better off to be never said for simply being useless in the large scheme of things.

I walked back into my dark room and sat on the bed. I could still feel my heart beating. I was cold with just my underwear on, my feet cold on the floor, my hands cold from nervousness. Out the window it was still bright moon-light, and I knew the next day would be colder and that maybe winter would come on before it ever became true fall. And what I felt like was a spy – hollow and not forceful, not able to cause anything. And I wished for a moment that I was dead, too, that all three of us were. I thought about how small my mother seemed out in the hall with her body showing in the light, how she had not been strong or force-ful, and that she must've felt that way herself, and that we felt the same way at that moment, saw the same future alone in our rooms, in our beds. I tried to imagine that this was a help but could not quite do it. Then a car went down our street, and as it came in front of our house it blew its horn — two honks and then a very long one. I jumped up to the window and looked out. I thought it would be Warren Miller — I didn't think it would be anyone else. He wanted to come back, or he wanted her to come where he was, or he just wanted her to know he was out there, in his car, in the dark, riding around Great Falls thinking about her in a kind of panic. The horn changed sound as it got farther down the street, and I never saw the car — if it was Warren Miller's Oldsmobile or someone else who did not know us. I saw its taillights and that was all, heard the horn stop. Then I got in bed and tried to be calm. I listened to the night in our house. I thought I heard my mother's bare feet on the floor, moving, thought I heard her door shut down the hall. But I could not be sure of it. And then I went to sleep.

THE NEXT MORNING was cold, as I thought it would be. I turned on my radio and listened to the forecast, which said there would be wind out of the southwest before the day was over, and that it would stay clear, though along the Rocky Mountain front snow was expected to offer relief for the crews fighting the Allen Creek fire.

I could hear my mother in the kitchen. She was wearing shoes that scraped the linoleum floor, and I knew she was going out soon. The air base, I thought, or to the grain elevator, or to Warren Miller's house. Anything still seemed possible. For some reason I thought I'd be leaving. I didn't have a place to go, or any place I wanted to go, but I realized I had waked up thinking, 'What am I going to do now?' And that seemed like a thought you had before you left someplace, even if it was a place you had always lived or the people you had always lived with.

My mother was sitting at the kitchen table when I got dressed and came out into the house. She was eating a piece of toast and a scrambled egg on a plate and drinking coffee. She looked worn out, though she was dressed in a nice way—a white blouse with a white bow up to her neck and a brown skirt and high heels. She looked at me, then looked at the clock on the stove which said it was ten fifteen, then went on eating her breakfast.

'Drink some coffee, Joe,' she said. 'Get a cup. You'll feel like a white person in a minute.'

I took a cup down and poured coffee out of the pot. My cheekbone hurt where she had hit me, but there wasn't a bruise I could see. I sat down across from her. I didn't think she would talk about last night, and I was not going to bring it up. It was all clear enough to me.

'What're you about to do now?' she said. She seemed very calm, as if something had stopped bothering her that had bothered her very much.

'I'm not going to school today,' I said.

'Okay,' she said. 'I didn't expect you'd go. I understand.'

'What are you going to do?' I drank some black coffee. I had not drunk much coffee before that, and it seemed too hot and not to have any taste to it.

'I'm going over to those Helen Apartments and rent a place,' she said. 'It'll have two bedrooms. You're welcome to live there.'

'All right,' I said. I didn't think she wanted me to, though it was not because she didn't love me. It just wasn't the first thing in her thinking that morning.

I sat at the table and tried to imagine what I could say to her, something that we could talk about together, anything ordinary about the future or even that day, but there didn't seem to be anything. She looked out the window toward the backyard, where the sky was visible—blue and with no clouds in it—then she drank some more coffee, picked up her fork and put it on her plate.

'Can I tell you something?' she said, and sat up straighter.

'Yes,' I said.

'You're going to have all these other mornings in your life when you wake up and nobody'll tell you how to feel,' she said very slowly. 'You'll just have to know. So would you let me tell you how to feel this time? I won't tell you any more. I promise.'

'Okay,' I said. And I was willing to do that. It was the thing I didn't know how to do at that moment, and I was glad she thought she did know.

My mother put the tips of her fingers on the edge of her plate where there were only some crumbs left and her dull silver fork. She looked at me and narrowed her lips. 'I haven't lost my mind yet,' she said. She looked away from me then as if she was hearing those words and thinking about the ones she was going to say next. 'You don't want to think when people do things you don't like that they're crazy. Because mostly they aren't. It's just that you're not part of it. That's all. And maybe you want to be.' She smiled at me and nodded as if she wanted me to agree with her.

'All right,' I said. 'I understand that,' and I did.

'I know you don't want to have this conversation with me,' she said. 'I'm sorry. I don't blame you. But I'm still alive. I haven't died. You have to get used to that. You have to account for everything. We all do.'

'Are you going to see Warren Miller today,' I asked.

And this was a question I wish I hadn't asked, because I didn't really care what the answer would be, and she had something she thought was better on her mind because she said, 'Christ almighty.' She got up and took her plate to the sink and ran water on it. 'The sky's falling,' she said. She leaned to the side and looked out the window at the morning sky. 'That's what you think, isn't it?' Her back was to me.

'No,' I said.

'I couldn't stand it to be young again,' she said. 'I'd run

III

from the fountain of youth, I swear to God. Yes, I'm going to see Warren. Or I guess I will. I don't know. Is that okay? I guess it's not.'

'Do you love him?' I said.

'Yes,' my mother said. 'And if you wonder how all that happens so fast, it simply does. So. Maybe it'll be over in a hurry.'

I wanted to ask if she loved my father and if it was possible to love two people at once. Though I knew what she thought the answer was; it was yes in both cases. And I thought she was probably right and wished there was something else she could say or I could to make just this moment better or more like a moment from the life I knew before.

'It isn't that you can't say no to somebody else, or somebody's just too good-looking,' my mother said. She was still looking out the window. 'You can't say no to yourself. It's a lack in you. Not somebody else. That's very clear to me.'

She looked at me over her shoulder just to see what my face looked like, or if I was about to say something or wanted her to say something else. But I must've seemed not to be thinking about that because she smiled at me and looked back out the window, just as if we were both waiting for something to happen. And I suppose in retrospect we were. We were waiting for my father to be there, and the fire to be controlled and for all our lives to become whatever they'd be from then on – different and maybe better or maybe worse.

'Be kind to me,' my mother said. 'Would you be kind to me? I know it'll make everything better. You can think bad things, but don't say them.'

'Yes, I will,' I said.

She turned as though she was going to go back to the bedroom. But she reached toward me as she did, and patted me on my shoulder. She said, 'You're a sweet boy. You're like your father.'

She left me in the kitchen and went into her room to get

herself ready to leave. I still wanted to ask her if she loved my father. I thought I would have an easier time being kind to her if I knew that. But sitting at the kitchen table there, alone, I didn't feel like I could shout it out, and didn't want to go into her room again. So I had to make myself satisfied with not knowing, since we never talked about that subject afterward.

After a few minutes, she came back through the kitchen on her way out. She had brushed her hair and put on lipstick and perfume. She was wearing a red winter coat and had found her purse and the car keys where I had hung them beside the door the night before. She came to where I was still sitting at the table, looking at the headlines on the front page of the *Tribune* without really reading them, and she put her arms around my neck and she hugged me hard and quickly. I could smell the perfume on her neck. Her face felt hard against my face, and she had been smoking a cigarette that morning. She said, 'Your life doesn't mean what you have, sweetheart, or what you get. It's what you're willing to give up. That's an old saying, I know. But it's still true. You need to have something to give up. Okay?'

'What if you don't want to give up anything?' I said.

'Oh, well. Good luck. You have to.' She smiled and kissed me again. 'That's really not one of the choices. You have to give things up. That's the rule. It's the major rule for everything.'

She went out the back door and across the cold yard toward whatever else the day would be likely to bring her way.

When she had been gone for a while and I'd finished reading the newspaper, I went back and got in my bed and tried to read my book on throwing the javelin, looked at the drawings of muscular men in all stages of the throw, but I couldn't make myself think about that. And then I thought I should go to sleep again because when I woke up I would have to think about what I was going to do. I believed I would probably leave town that day, and that my mother and I had said good-bye but hadn't exactly known it. Though I did not want to hurry, inasmuch as I didn't know where to go at all, or how I would get there, or if I would ever come back. And that seemed in itself like a loss – not the leaving, but having to decide where to go and how to get there and what it all would cost me. The details were the loss. And I thought I knew what my mother meant by what she'd said about giving things up, and that she was right. And what I thought about as I fell asleep in my bed late in that morning was loss and how I would get along with it alone and what I had of myself that I was willing to lose.

When I woke up again it was three o'clock. I had slept five hours and missed all of school for that day. I felt like I might not be going to school anymore and not to college either. I didn't see how that could be, but I felt it was, and I would not be surprised if someone said as much to me soon. And I felt that maybe the best part of my life was over for me now, and other things were starting. I was almost seventeen.

I took a shower and put on clean clothes. It was cold in the house, and I went into the kitchen and turned the furnace up, and looked for some sign that my mother had been in the house again. Her plate was still in the sink and her coffee cup was on the countertop the way they had been. Out the back window in the yard, red-winged blackbirds were sitting all across the grass. My mother's car was not in front of the house, though down Eighth, farther down than where it had been the night before and almost hidden behind our side hedge, Warren Miller's pink Oldsmobile was sitting against the curb. No one was in it. Though even as I was looking, Warren Miller himself walked, limping, out from behind the hedge and up the sidewalk toward the front of our house, and through the gate and up our walk as if he was coming right in the house, just as if my mother was there waiting for him.

I stepped to the side of the door, and reached across and under and turned the lock closed. I could hear Warren Miller's heavy steps on the porch as he came to the door. The ceiling light was on in the kitchen, and I knew he could see it and would think someone was inside. But I didn't move, though my heart started to pound fast. I stayed with my face against the wall while Warren turned the bell on the door, turned it twice, and waited. I could see just part of him through the window glass, the front of his coat. I heard his feet move, heard the change jingle in his pockets. He took a coin out of his pocket and tapped it on the glass, and said, 'Jenny, hon, are you inside? Are you inside there?' He waited a few seconds, then turned the doorknob to walk in, but the lock stopped him. He pushed it twice and pulled it back – not hard, but firmly. I was no more than a foot from him, though the wall was between us. I heard him say, 'Lord, Lord, Lord.' Then he walked off the porch.

I looked around the window frame at him. He was walking around toward the side of our house. I turned and hurried back through the kitchen in my sock feet and locked the back door before he could get to it. Then I went back into the hall, exactly where I had seen him the night before when he hadn't seen me. I listened to him tap on the door glass with his coin, then try the knob there, then go to the kitchen window and try it and find out it was locked. I heard him call my mother's name again. Not in a frantic voice, but an insistent one, as though he knew I was inside hiding from him, in my own house, and wouldn't let him in. I stayed in the hall listening while the furnace went on and off, heard him come to my mother's window and try it, then heard him try my window. But both of them were locked.

He tapped on my window. I knew he could see that my bed was not made, and that a towel from the bathroom was on the floor, and my shoes were there. I knew he knew I was there, and for that reason he might just break the glass and come in. But he didn't. He tried my window again, tapped on it, then it was quiet from all I could hear in the shadowy hallway. I stood and listened, tried to hear his limping walk. But I couldn't, though in a minute I thought I heard his car start down the street, heard the motor rev up high as if by accident. Then I heard nothing, no car sound, no sound at the door, no footsteps limping. And I thought he had finally gone away.

I walked down the hall and looked into my mother's room, where I had not wanted to go. The bed was made up. There was a pillow on the floor and clothes pushed out of the closet, and the curtains were shut so that the room was shadowy and cool. The clock said that it was three forty-five in the afternoon. I walked into the room and turned on the ceiling light. And what I saw on the floor near the end of the bed was a pair of socks, gray and red nylon ones turned almost inside out and – it looked to me – thrown there maybe from the bed. I walked over and picked them up, then looked around the floor to see what else there might be. I looked under the pillow and under the bed, but didn't see anything else – nothing that Warren Miller would want back or that my mother might want hidden. I took the socks into the kitchen and wrapped them in the newspaper that was on the table. Then I put the bundle in the trash under the sink and took the paper bag of trash out behind the house to the metal garbage can and put it in and went back in the house to put on my coat so I could go out into the town.

And then for a while I walked out into Great Falls.

It was late afternoon, and I knew it would not be light much longer, and that it would turn cold once the light had fallen, and I would not want to be out then but would want to be someplace else: on a bus going away from there, or in a hotel room in another town, or at home with my mother waiting for whatever would happen to us next. I did not know what that could possibly be.

Great Falls was a town where I did not know the streets well, so that I walked first to my school on Second Street, where there were still people inside and the lights were on even though school was out for the day. Boys were running on the track at the south end of the building, and the football team was scattered on the long playing field in their white practice jerseys, going through their drills in the chill breeze. I waited and watched them, listened to the sounds of clapping and shoulder pads hitting and their voices until I thought I might be noticed on the sidewalk at the edge of the grass. Someone would remember I'd played for a while and that I'd quit. And I didn't want to think about what someone else thought. So I walked all the way down Second Avenue North to the park by the river, then down the stream past the tennis courts and the archery targets to the Fifteenth Street Bridge and out onto the pedestrians' walk, where I took the clasp knife Warren Miller had given me — two days before, though it seemed like a month — and dropped it over the rail to where I couldn't see it strike the flat water.

From the bridge I could see the silver oil refinery tanks and the light towers at the baseball field where the Great Falls team played. I could see the fairgrounds and the smelter stack and the hot-rod course in Black Eagle, and the three white elevators Warren Miller owned or at least had an interest in, and where my mother said she wanted to work or had already worked or soon would if any of that was a true story. And beyond were the open prairies, flat and treeless as far away as I could see, all the way to Minneapolis and St. Paul, my father had told me.

Below the bridge two men were fishing, two tall Negroes

standing on the dry flats casting spinner spoons into the current. Two young white women sat on the grass on a blanket watching them, talking and laughing. The women had on slacks. No one was catching fish, and it did not seem to me like a good day to catch fish. The men were from the air base, I thought, and today was their time off. I doubted if they cared about the fish. They cared about the girls who, I thought, were town girls or Air Force girls, or nurses at the hospital, or waitresses who had their own days off together and were spending it this way, with these men. They seemed to be enjoying themselves.

I walked back up Fifteenth Street, under the trees that lined it, all the way to Tenth Avenue South and turned east and walked away from town. I thought that I would walk as far as the air base fence and watch the bombers take off toward the DEW Line or the Pacific—wherever they went. It was a thing I'd done with my father the spring before, after work, the big planes only lighted shadows that shot ahead of their big noises and disappeared into the stars and night.

Now seemed to be a time—the first one in my life—when I needed to know exactly what to do, and out of all the choices I had I wanted to choose the right thing, and start in that direction. So as I walked out the busy street past the air base strip joints and the car dealerships and the motels with their winter rates already on display, I began to arrange my thinking. My mother was going to marry Warren Miller soon; we would live in another house in Great Falls, and my father would probably move away to some other town, back to Lewiston, maybe. I understood why she liked Warren: because he knew things. He knew more things than my father did, and he was older. I wondered if there had been other men in my mother's life before, or other women in my father's, people I didn't know about. But I decided that there hadn't been because I would have known it—being there as I was all the time, with them. And then I wondered what would happen if my father had an accident where he was, or lost his memory, or never came back home. How would that be? Or if my mother didn't come home today and I never saw her again. Would anyone understand anything then?

When I got to Thirty-eighth Street, I crossed over to the south side and walked along the bar fronts there. Cars were parking in front of the bars, and men and women were getting out to go in and drink. Behind the bars were sheds and then rows of small new houses built on new streets, and beyond that an empty drive-in movie and a railroad spur and then the town stopped and the fields of winter wheat began.

So, I wondered, were my mother and father separated now? Was that what this meant? My father leaves the house. My mother has another man come to visit her. I knew you could know the words but not match them with the life. But to be able to do it right said something about you. And I didn't know if my judgment was good enough, or exactly what was good or bad. Though there must be times, I thought, when there was no right thing to *know*, just as there were times when there was no right thing to do. 'Limbo' was the word my mother had used, and that is where I was now – in limbo, between the cares of other people with only my own cares to show me what to do.

I had walked as far as the base fence, which was across Tenth Avenue. Beyond it were apartments and the golf course where my father had taught lessons, and then the wide landing strip and the control tower and the flat low buildings of the base. Light was going out of the sky in the east. One jet took off as I watched, and the day seemed gray and over with. In an hour it would be full dark and much colder, and I would want to be at home.

On the side of the street toward town was a bar called the Mermaid, and cars were there, and on the roof was a neon sign with a green mermaid shining in the dull afternoon light. It was a place where airmen went, and my father had taken me there on the days he'd taught golf at the base. I knew what it was like inside there now, knew what color the light was, how the air smelled, knew the voices of the airmen – low and soft as if they knew secrets. As I walked past the bar a black Mercury drove in and parked, and the two Negroes I had seen fishing an hour ago, back in town, were inside. Their car, I saw, had a tag from another state – a yellow tag – and they were alone. The white girls who had been with them were gone, and the men were laughing as they got out. One put his long arm around the other man's shoulders. 'Oh, I couldn't help it. No, no,' he said, 'I couldn't help myself.' They both laughed again, and the one who had talked looked at me and smiled as they walked past me, and said, 'Don't worry, son, we're not going to kill anybody in here.' Then they both laughed out loud and went inside the door to the Mermaid and disappeared.

And then I began to walk home. I had wanted to leave that day, but I saw that I couldn't, because my parents were there still and I was too young. And even though I couldn't help them by staying, we belonged together in some way I couldn't change. I remembered as I walked through the cold evening toward the rising lights of Great Falls, a town that was not my home and never would be, that my mother had asked me in the middle of the night before if I had a plan for her. And I didn't have a plan, though if I'd had one it would be that both of them could live longer than I would and be happier than I was. Death was less terrible at that moment than being alone, even though I was not alone and hoped I wouldn't be, and even though it was a childish thought. I realized at that moment that I was crying and didn't know I was, wouldn't have guessed it. I was only walking home, I thought, trying to think about things, all the things in my life, just as they were.

WHEN I GOT HOME it was dark. The moon had gone behind clouds and I was cold as I came up the walk because I had not dressed warmly. Lights were on in our house, and up and down our street. Tiny mists of snow, the first snow of the year, were drifting onto the yard. It would not stay long, I guessed, though I didn't know when winter truly started.

My mother was sitting on the couch—in the middle of it—in the living room, playing a card game by herself. It was a game I had seen her play before and it required two decks. She'd learned it in college. She was dressed the way she had been that morning—her white blouse with a white bow, a brown skirt and high heels. She looked nice to me. She was sitting on the front edge of the couch, with the cards laid out on the low coffee table, and her knees to the side. She looked like somebody who was going somewhere.

She looked up and smiled when I came inside and shut the door. She had half of the cards in her hand. I did not see a drink anywhere.

'Where have you been till after dark,' she said, 'and half undressed on top of that?'

'I went to work,' I said. It was another lie, but I didn't think it mattered and didn't want to say I had walked as far as the air base.

'Did you go to school?' she said, still looking at me.

'No,' I said.

'Well, you can later, I guess. I thought you might go after lunch.'

'Where were you today?' I said. I sat down on the chair that was beside the TV. My arms were cold, but it was warm inside. I wondered what there was in the house to eat. I had forgotten about eating.

'I went to the Helen,' she said. 'Then I had some other things to do.'

'Are you going to rent one of those?' I said.

My mother divided the cards she was holding into two stacks and put one on top of the other. 'I paid some out on one this morning,' she said. 'It seemed nice. You'd like it.'

'Did you see Warren Miller?'

My mother put her cards down and sat back on the couch and looked at me. 'I'm waiting for your father to come home,' she said. And this was no surprise. I'd thought my father would be home that day if he wasn't dead. He hadn't said so, but it was just something I knew about both of them – the intervals it took them to do things. I knew them that well. 'Did you happen,' my mother said, 'to find a pair of striped socks anywhere in this house today?'

'No,' I said.

'Well.' She smiled. 'Have you eaten anything?'

'No,' I said. 'But I'm hungry.'

'I'd fix something,' she said. Then she looked around at the clock that was beside the door to the kitchen. 'I'll fix something in a little while,' she said. 'Your father's coming in a cab. I thought you might be him driving up.'

I looked out the window behind me and saw only the snow seeming to dance in a new wind, and the empty sidewalk, and the lights in the houses across Eighth Street. I thought our car must be in the garage now, and that my mother had been at Warren Miller's house all day. Maybe she had been to the Helen Apartments for an hour, but she had gone to Warren's after that. She didn't care if I knew it. She may have felt like she had slipped off the world and, while we waited for my father to arrive, been waiting to hit the ground again. There was a way in which I felt that, too, and felt sorry for her.

'It snowed up there where they were today,' she said quietly. 'And now it's snowing down here.' It was just a thing to say, to make waiting not be uncomfortable.

'I know it,' I said.

'Did you think your father would be injured?'

'No,' I said. 'I hoped he wouldn't be.'

'Me too,' my mother said. 'That's the truth.' She folded her arms and looked across the room at the front windows. 'I have passion for him. I feel that. But I don't feel I have the way to express it now. I guess that's it. That's the problem.' She ran her fingers back through her brown hair and cleared her throat. I could see she had a little mark on her neck, like a little bruise, something she touched with her finger without realizing it. 'Events can maroon you more than people can. I know that,' she said, and breathed out. 'Do you feel that way, Joe? Don't you feel marooned out here?'

'No,' I said. 'I don't.'

'That's good,' my mother said. 'I guess you have a lot to look forward to.'

She stood up. She was watching out the front window. She brushed her hand over the front of her skirt and pushed her hair back again. I looked at her, then looked around.

Outside at the curb beyond our wooden fence was a yellow cab, its red roof light shining in the snowy evening. The interior light was on, and I could see the driver turned back, talking to someone who I knew was my father. I saw my father's hand with money in it and saw the driver laugh at something they were saying. Then the back door opened and my father got out, holding the gladstone bag he'd left with. It seemed like a long time ago to me.

'Well. There comes the firefighter,' my mother said. She was standing, looking out the porch window from in front of the couch. She had her arms crossed and was standing very straight.

I got up out of my chair and opened the front door. The porch light was on. I went down the steps to meet my father, who was halfway up the walk, and put my arms around him. He looked larger than he had two days ago, and he was smiling. His black hair had been cut short and his face was dirty and unshaven. He put his bag down and put his arms around me. He had on a heavy canvas shirt and canvas pants and black logger's boots, and when my face was against his clothes what he smelled like was ashes and things that had been burned. His shirt was stiff and dirty and rough against my face. I heard the cab drive away. He put his hand on my neck, and it was cold and hard. 'It started to snow,' he said, 'so they sent the smart people home. How are you doing down here?' His voice seemed clipped, and he hugged me again, harder. It seemed silly in a way, because he had not been gone very long.

'That's good,' I said.

'Is your mother still walking on her lip?'

'I don't know,' I said. I held on to him a moment. 'I don't know,' I said again.

'Well, we'll have to see, I guess,' he said. He picked up his bag. 'Let's get out of the snow. You'd think we were in Montana here.' We walked, the two of us, up the porch steps and into the house, where it was warm and the lights were all turned on and my mother was waiting.

She was sitting back on the couch facing the front door, where she'd been when I came home, though she was not playing cards. The cards were all in two decks in front of her on the table. She smiled at him when we came in, but she didn't stand up. And I knew that surprised him. It was not what he thought would happen, and it must have let him down and let him know that something was not usual.

'How was the fire?' was all my mother said. 'Did you put it out?'

'No,' my father said. He was smiling. I think he must've known he was.

'I could've guessed,' she said. And then she smiled at him again, and got up off the couch and came across the living room and kissed him, put her hands on his arms and kissed him on the cheek. I was standing right beside them. When she had kissed him she said, 'I'm glad to see you back, Jerry. Joe is, too.' Then she walked away from him and me, and sat back down on the couch.

'I feel like I've been gone a long time,' my father said.

'Three days is all,' my mother said. She looked as if she was still smiling, but she wasn't. 'Have you eaten any dinner?'

'No,' my father said, 'but I'm not hungry.' He stood for a moment holding his black suitcase. I thought one of them would tell me to leave the room, to go do something for myself, but they didn't. And I just stood beside the front door feeling a draft seep in over the sill and across my ankles.

'Why don't you sit down?' my mother said. 'You must be tired. You must've seen a lot of different things.'

'I don't know who I'm waiting to impress here,' my father said, and set his bag down behind the front door and sat where I had been sitting, in the armchair beside the television. I could see him better. He moved stiffly. The backs of his hands were hard, as if they had been baked, and I could still smell the ash smell that was on him. It was a smell I hadn't associated with a person before I had smelled it at the cafe where my mother and I had eaten two nights before.

'You don't have to impress me,' my mother said. 'That's for sure.'

'Did you think I'd be killed?' my father said.

'I hoped you wouldn't be,' my mother said. She smiled at him then in a way to make you think she liked him. 'We'd have been disappointed here at home,' she said. 'Will the fire ever go out?'

My father looked at his hands, where they were red and sore-looking. 'It'll smoke and smolder on for a long time. It's hard to put out.'

'I had a mystical feeling while you were gone,' my mother said, and I could see her relax a little. I thought that maybe things were going to be fine now, and there wouldn't be trouble. 'I thought,' she said, 'that maybe the whole fire was a thing not to be put out at all. And you men just—everybody—went there to invigorate yourselves.'

'That's not exactly right,' my father said. He looked up at me. His eyes were red and small and tired. But he looked fine, and maybe he was invigorated the way my mother had said. There didn't seem anything wrong with that. 'It takes you outside yourself is what it does,' he said. 'You see everything from outside. You're up against so big a thing out there.' He looked up at me again and at my mother, and he blinked his eyes. 'Everything seems arbitrary. You step outside your life and everything seems like something you choose. Nothing seems very natural. It's probably hard to understand. I saw flames a hundred feet high suddenly just turn sideways like a blowtorch. Just go out of kilter. A man got blown off his horse just from air blowing past him.' My father shivered, as though a fright had passed through him.

And he shook his head quickly as if he wanted to shake a picture out of it.

'That's awful,' my mother said.

'I feel strange now,' my father said. 'But I'm glad to be home.'

'I'm glad you came,' my mother said. She looked at me in a way I thought was confused. She was making a decision. And though I knew what I wished she would decide, I didn't have the nerve to say so, to try to help her. They had things to say to each other that I had nothing to do with. 'How did it all start?' she said then. 'Do they know how that happened?'

'Arson,' my father said, and sat back in his chair. 'A man did it. I wouldn't want to be him. Somebody'll kill him, I know that. It may have been an Indian.'

'Why would you think that?' my mother said.

'I just don't like them,' my father said. 'They leave their own behind, and they're secretive. I don't like to trust them.'

'I see,' my mother said.

'What about school?' my father said to me then, and turned toward me. He seemed to need to turn his whole body when he did. Probably he had been sleeping on the ground, is what I thought, and ached from it.

'He's doing fine at that,' my mother said before I could answer. I think she didn't want me to lie to him, and she knew that I was about to. The truth wouldn't have helped anything then.

'That's good.' My father smiled at me. 'I guess I haven't been gone that long, have I?'

'You've been gone long enough,' my mother said. And for a moment neither of them said anything.

'A man talked to me today about a job with the Forestry. The foresters,' my father said. He was not paying much attention to my mother. He was feeling better about things, I think. 'A college degree is a plus with them. Experience isn't so important. They'll provide us a house up in Choteau.'

'Jerry, I have something I have to tell you,' my mother said. She sat forward on the edge of the couch, with her knees together and her hands on her skirt. My father stopped talking about the Forestry and looked at her. He could tell something was important, though I don't think he had any idea what it might be. That my mother would leave him was the last thing he could've had on his mind. I think he might've thought things were going to be better. He had a right to think that, really.

'Tell me what it is, Jean,' he said. 'I'm just running on here. I'm sorry.'

'I'm going to move into another place. I'm going to move in tomorrow,' my mother said, and her voice seemed louder than it needed to be. She looked as though she had just said something she hadn't understood herself, and that had scared her. It is probably not how she thought she would feel.

'What do you mean by that?' my father said. 'What in the world?' He was staring at her.

'It's a surprise, I know,' my mother said. 'I'm surprised myself.' She had not moved, had kept her knees together and her hands very still on her lap.

'Are you crazy?' my father said.

'No,' my mother said very quietly. 'I don't think I am.'

My father suddenly turned and looked out the front window. It was as if he thought someone was there, outside on the porch or in the yard or the street, watching him, somebody he could have reference to, somebody who could give him an idea about what was happening to him. The street was empty, of course. Snow was coming down through the streetlamp light.

He turned and looked at my mother again, quickly. He had forgotten about me. They both had. My father's face was pale.

'I'm coming down with something,' he said, and he clenched his fist on the arm of the chair. 'Probably a cold.' My mother just stared at him. 'Are you stepping out on me?' he said. He tapped his fist on the chair arm as if he was nervous.

My mother looked at me. Maybe she didn't even want to have to go through with anything now. But she had gone too far, and I don't think she saw any choice. 'Well,' she said. 'Yes. I am.'

'Who is it?' my father said.

'Oh, just somebody I like,' my mother said.

'Somebody from the country club?' my father said. He was getting furious, and my mother must've felt she couldn't stop it now.

'Yes,' she said. 'But that's not what it's about. That's just a circumstance.'

'I know that,' my father said. 'I believe that.' He got up and walked around the room. It was as if he wanted to hear his feet hit the floor, hear the loud noise his boots made on the wood. He walked around behind the couch, then back into the middle of the room. I could smell him, the ashy smell, and I knew my mother could too. Then he sat back down in the chair by the television.

'I don't know what makes life hold together at all,' he said. He did not seem as mad now, only very unhappy. I felt sorry for him.

'I know,' my mother said. 'I don't either. I'm sorry.'

My father squeezed his hands together tightly in front of him. 'What in the hell are you thinking about, Jean?' He looked up at me then. 'I don't even care who it is.' He said this to me, for some reason.

'It's Warren Miller,' my mother said flatly.

'Well, good for him then,' my father said.

'Your attitude toward things changes,' my mother said.

'I know that,' my father said. 'I'm aware of that.'

My mother put her hands down beside her on the couch.

It was the first time she had moved in several minutes. She must've thought the worst part of this time was over with, and it's possible that for her it was.

'I don't want you to be mad at me,' my father said, 'just because I went to a fire. Do you understand?'

'I understand,' my mother said. 'I'm not mad at you.'

'Love is one thing,' my father said. And then he just stopped talking. He looked all around the room for an instant as if something had startled him, something he heard or expected to hear, or just something he thought of while he was talking that made the rest of what he was about to say fly out of his mind. 'Where are you going to move to?' he said. 'Are you moving in with Miller?'

'The Helen Apartments,' my mother said. 'They're down by the river. On First.'

'I know where they are,' my father said abruptly. Then he said, 'Christ almighty, it's hot in here, Jean.' His canvas shirt was buttoned all the way to the top, and he suddenly unbuttoned three buttons right down to the middle of his chest. 'You should turn it down in here,' he said. I remembered that I was the one who had turned the furnace up earlier that day when I had been alone in the house and cold.

'That's true,' my mother said. 'I'm sorry.' But she did not get up. She stayed where she was.

'Have you had a hard three days?' my father said.

'No,' my mother said. 'Not very hard.'

'Good, then.' My father looked at her. 'Are we not getting along? Is that it?'

'I think so,' my mother said calmly. She touched her neck with her fingers. The mark was below her collar and the white bow, but she must've just become aware of it and wondered where it was and if he could see it, which he couldn't. He knew nothing about it.

'I'd certainly like to see the world the same way again. Have things be all right.' My father said this and smiled at her. 'I feel like everything's tilting. The whole works.'

'I've felt that way,' my mother said.

'Boy,' my father said. 'Boy, boy.' He shook his head and smiled. I know he was amazed to have all this happening to him. He had never dreamed that it could. Maybe he was trying to think what he had done wrong, go back in time to when life was set straight. But he couldn't think of when that was.

'Jerry,' my mother said. 'Why don't you go out and take Joe for something to eat. I didn't cook tonight. I didn't know you were coming till too late.'

'That's a good idea,' my father said. He looked at me and smiled again. 'This is a wild life, isn't it son?' he said.

'He doesn't know what is and isn't.' My mother said this crossly, in a scolding way, without any sympathy for him. She got up and stood behind the table with the decks of cards on it. She was waiting for us to leave.

'I think I'm wasted on you,' my father said. He was angry again in just that instant. I didn't blame him.

'I think you are, too,' my mother said. And she smiled in a way that was not a smile. She just wanted this moment in her life to be over, and for something else – probably any-thing – to happen next. 'We're all wasted on everything nowadays,' she said. Then she turned and walked out of the living room, leaving us in it all alone, just me and my father with no place to go but out into the night, and no one to be with but each other.

WE DROVE DOWN TO Central Avenue to where there were cafes and some bars I could get a meal in. It had gone on snowing in tiny flakes that swirled in front of the headlights, but the pavement was already damp and shining with water, and the snow had begun to turn to rain by the time we were downtown, so that it seemed more like spring in eastern Washington than the beginning of winter in Montana.

In the car my father acted like things weren't so bad. He told me he would take me to a movie if I wanted to go to one, or that we could go stay in a hotel for the night. The Rainbow, he'd heard, was a good place. He mentioned that the Yankees were playing well in the World Series so far, but that he hoped Pittsburgh would win. He also said that bad things happened and adults knew it, but that they finally passed by, and I should not think we were all just an accumulation of our worst errors because we were all better than we thought, and that he loved my mother and she loved him, and that he had made mistakes himself and that we all deserved better. And I knew he believed he would make life right between them again.

'Things can surprise you. I'm aware of that,' he said to me as we drove down Central in the cold car. 'When I was in Choteau I saw a moose, if you can believe that. Right down in the middle of town. The fire had driven it out of where it normally roamed. Everybody was amazed.'

'What happened to it?' I said.

'Oh, I don't know that,' my father said. 'Some of them wanted to shoot it but some others didn't. I didn't hear about it later. Maybe it did okay.'

We drove down to the end of Central and parked in front of a bar that had bright lights inside, and walls that were painted white and very high ceilings. It was called The Presidential, and I could see through the windows from the street that men were playing cards at two tables in the back, but no one was at the bar drinking. I had looked into this bar on my walks through town and thought that railroad men went there because it was near the train stations and the railroad hotels. 'This is a fine place here,' my father said. 'They have good food and you can hear yourself think a thought.'

The bar was a long, narrow room and had framed pictures of two or three presidents on the wall. Roosevelt was one. Lincoln was another. We sat at the bar, and I ordered navy bean soup and a pasty pie. My father ordered a glass of whiskey and a beer. I had not eaten since morning and I was hungry, though as I sat at the bar with my father I couldn't help wondering what my mother was doing. Was she packing her suitcase? Was she talking on the telephone to Warren Miller or to someone else? Was she sitting on her bed crying? None of those seemed exactly right. And I decided that when I had eaten my meal, I would ask my father to take me back home. He would understand someone wanting to do that, I thought, especially for your mother, at a bad time.

'A lot of what's burned, you know, is just understory.' My father's hand was on his glass of whiskey, and he was looking at the scarred skin on the back of it. 'You'll be able to go in there next spring. You'll live in a house one of these days made of that timber. A fire's not always such a bad thing.' He looked at me and smiled.

'Were you afraid out there,' I asked. I was eating my pasty pie.

'Yes, I was. We only were digging back trenches, but I was afraid. Anything can go on. If you had an enemy he could kill you and no one would know it. I had to stop a man from running straight into the fire once. I dragged him down.' My father took a drink of his beer and rubbed one hand over the other one. 'Look at my hands,' he said. 'I had smooth hands when I played golf.' He rubbed his hand harder. 'Are you proud of me now?' he said.

'Yes,' I said. And that was true. I had told my mother that I was, and I was.

I heard poker chips clatter in the back of the room and a chair squeak as someone got up. 'You can't quit now, I'm winning,' someone said and people laughed.

'I'd like to live up on the eastern front,' my father said. 'That would be a nicer life than down here. Get out of Great Falls.' His mind was just running then; whatever he thought, he said. It was a strange night in his life.

'I'd like to live up there,' I said, though I had never been closer to the eastern front than when I had gone with my mother two days before, and everything there had been on fire.

'Do you think your mother would take a chance on it?' he said.

'She might,' I said. My father nodded, and I knew he was thinking about the eastern front, someplace where it was not likely he'd be suited for things and my mother wouldn't be either. They'd lived in houses in towns all their lives and made good with that. He was just taking his mind off the things that he didn't like and couldn't help.

My father ordered another glass of whiskey but no beer. I asked for a glass of milk and piece of pie. He turned around on his stool and looked at the men in the back who were playing cards. No one else was in the bar. It was seven o'clock and people would not come in until later when shifts let off.

'I guess I should've known about all this happening,' my father said, facing the other way. 'There's always someone else involved somewhere. Even if it's just in your mind. You can't control your mind, I know that. Probably you shouldn't try.' I sat without saying anything because I thought he was going to ask me something I did not want to answer. 'Has this been going on for some time?' my father said.

'I don't know,' I said.

'You get into these things and they seem like your whole life,' my father said. 'You can't see out of them. I'm understanding about that.'

'I don't know,' I said again.

'It's the money,' my father said. 'That's the big part of it. That's the way families break up. There's not enough money. I'm surprised about this Miller, though,' he said. 'He doesn't seem like a man who'd do that. I've played golf with him. He has a limp of some kind. I think I won some money once off him.'

'He said that,' I said.

'Do you know him?' And my father looked at me.

'I did meet him,' I said. 'I met him once.'

'Isn't he a married man himself?' my father said. 'I thought he was.'

'No,' I said. 'He isn't. He was.'

'When did you happen to meet him?' my father said.

And suddenly I felt afraid—afraid of my father, and of what I would say. Because I felt if I said the wrong thing something in me would be ruined and I would never be the same again. I wanted to get up from my seat at that instant and leave. But I couldn't. I was there with my father, and there was no place I could go that would be far enough away. And what I decided was that what people believed—that I knew nothing about my mother and Warren Miller, for example—didn't matter as much as it mattered what the truth was. And I decided that that's what I would tell if I had to tell anything and if I knew the truth, no matter what I'd thought before when I was not face to face with it.

Though I think that was the wrong thing to have done, and my father would have thought so too if he'd had the chance to choose, which he didn't. Only I did. It was because of me.

My father turned on the barstool and looked at me, his eyes small and hard-looking. He wanted me to tell him the truth. I knew that. But he did not know what the truth would be.

'I met him at our house,' I said.

'When did this take place,' my father asked.

'Yesterday,' I said. 'Two days ago.'

'What happened? What happened then?'

'Nothing,' I said.

'And you never met him again?' my father said.

'I met him at his house,' I said.

'Why did you go there?' My father was watching me. Maybe he hoped I was lying, and he would catch me at it, lying maybe to make my mother look worse, for some reason he imagined in which I would want to do something for him, to make him feel better by taking his side. 'Did you go to his house alone?'

'No,' I said. 'I went with Mother. We had our dinner over there.'

'You did?' he said. 'Did you stay all night?'

'No,' I said. 'We didn't. We left and went home.'

'And that's all?' he said.

'That was all then,' I said.

'But did you see your mother do something while I was gone that you wouldn't like to have to tell me?' my father said. 'I know it's odd to know about this. It's all probably my fault. I'm sorry.' He looked at me very hard. I think he didn't want me to say anything, but he also wanted to know the truth and what part in it I'd played, and what part in it my mother had, and what was right or wrong about it. And I did not say anything else because even though I could see it all in my mind again—all those things that had happened in just three days—I didn't think I knew everything and did not want to pretend I did, or that what I'd seen was the truth.

'Maybe it doesn't require an answer,' my father said after a while. He looked back at the men playing cards at the end of the room. 'Did your mother tell you anything?' my father said. 'I mean, did she say anything that you remember? Not about what she might've done. But just anything. I'd like to know what was on her mind.'

'She said she wasn't crazy,' I said. 'And she said it's hard to say no to yourself.'

'Those are both true,' my father said, watching the men play cards. 'I've felt those myself. Is that all?'

'She said everybody had to give up things.'

'Is that so?' my father said. 'That's good to know about. I wonder what she's given up?'

'I don't know,' I said.

'Maybe she's decided to give us up. Or just me. That's probably it.'

The bartender brought my pie and my milk and a fork. He set my father's glass of whiskey on the bar. But my father was looking the other way. He was thinking, and he sat that way without talking for a long time—maybe three minutes – while I sat beside him and waited and did not eat any of my pie or do anything. Just sat.

'I was only there for three days, but it did feel like a long time,' he finally said. 'I can certainly sympathize with people.'

'Yes,' I said. I touched my fork with my fingers.

But my father turned and looked at me again. 'I think you must have seen your mother with this Miller, didn't you? Not just about dinner, I mean.'

His voice was very calm, so I just said, 'Yes, I did.'

'Where were they?' my father said, looking at me.

'In the house,' I said.

'In our house?' he said.

'Yes,' I said. And I don't know why I told him that. He didn't make me do it. I just did. It must've seemed natural at that moment.

'Well, I'm sorry, Joe,' my father said. 'I know that wasn't what you expected.'

'It's all right,' I said.

'Well, no,' my father said. 'It's not all right. But it'll have to become all right with you somehow.'

He turned around away from me, then he picked up his glass of whiskey. 'I don't have to drink, but I just want to right now,' he said. He drank down a little of what he had and put it down. 'When you're finished with your pie,' he said, 'we'll go out for a ride.'

While I ate my pie, my father got up and went to the restroom. Then he came out and he made a phone call at the back of the bar. I watched him, but I couldn't hear what he said or who he was talking to. I thought possibly he was talking to my mother, talking about what I had just told him, maybe saying that he would not be bringing me home that night, or telling her to leave home herself, or how disappointed he was with her. I thought each of those things, though he did not talk long. When he came back, he had a five-dollar bill in his hand, and he put that on the bar and said to me, 'Let's clear our heads.' And we walked outside, where it was snowing lightly again. People were waiting in line down the street to go into the Auditorium. But he did not notice them and we got in the car and drove up Central away from downtown.

My father drove all the way out to Fifteenth Street. We did not talk much. He pulled into a gas station and got out, and I sat and listened as he talked to the man who filled up the car. They talked about the snow, which the attendant said would be turning to rain then ice, and about the fire in Allen Creek, which my father said he had been fighting until that very afternoon, and which he and the attendant both believed would now go out. The man checked the oil and the tires, then he opened the trunk to do something I couldn't see. He said something to my father about needing a new taillight, and then my father paid him and got in and we drove back out onto the street.

We drove down Central again to the middle of Great Falls by the train stations and the city park and the river where I'd already walked that day, and past the Helen Apartments where my mother was moving. My father did not seem to notice them, or to notice much of anything. He was just driving, I thought, with no particular destination while his mind was working on whatever he had to think about: my mother, me, what would happen to all of us. As we went father out toward the east, I could see the lights of the football stadium shining in the snowy sky. It was Friday night and a game was being played. Great Falls and Billings. I was glad not to be involved in it.

'I said a fire can be a good thing, didn't I?' my father said. 'Most people don't believe that.' He seemed in better spirits driving, as if he had thought of something that made him feel better. 'It's sure surprising how fast the world can turn backwards, isn't it?'

'Yes,' I said, 'it is.'

'Three days, if I'm not wrong,' he said. 'Maybe things were not as solid as I thought. I guess that's evident.'

'I don't know,' I said.

'Oh, sure,' he said. 'That's evident.' He looked at me, and he was smiling. He put his hand on my shoulder and could feel my bones. 'Joe,' he said, 'once you face it, the worst is all behind you. Things start to improve then. Going to the fire just had a bad effect on your mother. That's all.'

'Did you ever like being there?' I said. And this was something I'd wanted to know.

'Oh,' my father said. 'My attitude changed. First it was mysterious. Then it was exciting. Then I felt helpless about it. I felt bottled up before I went,' he said. 'I stopped feeling that way.'

'Did you have a girlfriend out there,' I asked, because that was what my mother had said two nights ago.

'No I didn't,' he said. 'There were women there. I saw women fight each other, in fact. I saw them fight like men.'

And that seemed strange to me – two women fighting. Though it was an exciting thought, and I realized how odd it was for me to talk this way with my father, and for us both to know what we knew about my mother and to feel the way we did about it, which was not so bad at all. It seemed like a reckless, exciting feeling to me, and I liked it.

'Does your mother's boyfriend live in Black Eagle on Prospect Street?' my father said as he drove along. Up ahead of us was the bridge to Black Eagle and beyond it the white grain elevators, lighted in the misting, snowy air. 'You said you were there, didn't you?'

'Yes,' I said.

'So you know where he lives?' my father said.

'Yes,' I said, 'that's where it is.'

'All right,' my father said. 'Let's go by there.'

He turned left onto the Fifteenth Street Bridge and we drove over the Missouri River and into Black Eagle, where there were only lights of houses against the bluff hills, and the snowy night up behind it like a curtain.

We drove halfway up the hill and turned right. It was eight o'clock at night, and many of the houses we passed had their porch lights on, and lights shining inside. My father seemed to know where he was going because he only looked now and then at the house numbers. Down the street I began to see the blue light of the Italian steakhouse. I could not see people in the street or any cars parked outside, and if it had not been Friday I would've thought it was closed.

'It's not a glamorous street, is it?' my father said.

'No, it isn't,' I said, watching the houses.

'That's surprising,' he said. 'I guess nobody sees through the eyes of a rich man.' He was quiet then for a moment as he drove slowly down Warren Miller's street. 'I wish I could get your mother to back out on this.'

'So do I,' I said.

'It's not a good deal for her,' he said. 'Not that I can see.'

He stopped the car across the street from Warren's house, in the place where my mother had parked the night before. I started to think what I had been thinking, sitting here with my mother: that I had no choice but to go inside with her when she went, and that I had gone. Then I stopped thinking that because it seemed like an entirely different subject now, one that had practically nothing to do with what had happened the night before, or any other night. I was with my father now, and everything was different.

Lights were on inside the house, though the porch was dark. Warren's Oldsmobile sat parked in the steep driveway, behind the powerboat, just as it had been. My father turned off the engine and opened the window and looked out at the house. I could hear piano music. I thought it was coming from Warren Miller's house, and that Warren was probably playing it as we sat in the dark watching.

'I'd like to have a look in there, I guess,' my father said. He turned and looked at me in the dark. 'What do you think about that?'

'Okay,' I said. I looked past him at the house, where I could see no one at the window where the old-fashioned lamp was burning.

'I'll come right back, Joe.'

'All right,' I said.

He got out of the car, closed the door, and walked across the street and up the concrete steps. I could hear the piano music playing out into the night, and thought I heard someone singing with it. A man. I thought no one would notice my father now unless he wanted them to or unless he rang the doorbell or knocked, and I didn't think he would do that. I wondered who my father had called from The Presidential bar. My mother? Or Warren Miller, to see if he was at home? Or possibly someone else entirely?

My father walked to the top of the steps and onto the porch. He turned around and looked at the car and then above it at the town lighted beyond the street of houses and the river. Then he walked to the front window and looked inside the house, bent over so he could see. He didn't try to hide, just stood in the window, looking, so that anybody who would've glanced at the window at that moment would've seen him.

He did not stay at the window long, just long enough to look around inside at the living room and at whatever he could see through there, the other rooms, the kitchen. Then he turned around and came back down the steps to the street and across to the car where I was sitting, waiting. He did not get in the car with me, only leaned in the window.

'How do you feel now, son?' he said. He looked in at me.

'I feel good,' I said, though that was not exactly how I felt. I felt nervous to be there, and I wished we could leave.

'Are you cold?' he said. He wasn't talking very loud.

'No sir,' I said. I could hear the piano still going inside the house. And I *was* cold. My arms were cold.

My father turned his head and looked down the street. There was nothing to see. No movement. 'Maybe I can't be in love anymore,' he said, then let out a breath. 'I'd love to improve things, though. You know?'

'Yes sir,' I said. Then I saw Warren Miller. He came right to the window where my father had been looking inside. He stopped a moment and stared out, I thought, at our car, then walked away. He was wearing a white shirt just the way he had the night before. I wondered if my mother was inside the house with him, and if that was what my father had seen when he looked and the reason he'd said what he'd just said. And I decided that she was definitely not inside there, and that she was still at home where we had left her and would find her again if we would just go back.

'Something's going to happen,' my father said, and he tapped his hands, both of them, on the metal window molding. He looked down at the street as if he was thinking. 'I wish I didn't feel that way.'

I didn't say anything for a moment, and then I said, 'So do I.'

My father breathed out a sigh again. 'I know that,' he said. 'I know that.' He was quiet for a moment himself while he looked down at the pavement. 'I just wonder,' he said, 'what would have to happen to make me ever leave your mother.' He looked up at me.

'Maybe nothing would,' I said.

'Nothing I can think of would. That's right.' He nodded. 'Things do have to be able to surprise you,' he said. 'This is an odd day, isn't it?' he said. 'It's an important day.'

'I guess it is,' I said.

'I feel exhausted by it,' he said. 'Just exhausted.'

And that is what I felt, too, and he must've known it. 'Maybe we should go back home now,' I said quietly to him.

143

'We should. We certainly should,' he said. 'We'll do that in a minute.'

He stood up then and walked to the back of the car and opened the trunk. I looked back, but I couldn't see what he was doing and did not hear anything. He didn't say anything that I could hear. He closed the trunk lid, and when I looked out the side window I saw him. He was hurrying up the concrete steps towards Warren Miller's white house, where the lights were on and piano music was coming out still. He was carrying something–I didn't know what, but something I thought he had taken out of the trunk of our car. He held it in both hands in front of him. And I had the feeling I have heard about since then that comes with disaster, the feeling of seeing things from a long way away, as if you were looking at them through a telescope backward, but they are right in front of you, only you are fixed there and helpless. It makes you feel cold, and then it makes you feel warm, as if what you're afraid of is not going to happen, only then it does and you are all the more unprepared to see it and have it happen to you.

What I saw was my father coming to the top of the steps and moving onto the little porch that ran partway along the front of the house. He turned and walked to the very end of the porch, right across in front of the window. I could hear his feet on the porch boards. I heard the faint sound of something being poured out of a bottle. And then I knew what he was doing, or trying to do. The music inside Warren Miller's house stopped. And it was quiet except for the sound of my father's boots and the noise of pouring out of a gallon jug, which is what he was holding. He was pouring whatever it was–the gasoline or the kerosene he had bought–out onto the house where the porch boards met the front wall. And I wanted to stop him, but he was moving fast, and I couldn't move fast enough in the car, just couldn't seem to work my hands fast or make a noise that would get his attention so I could tell him to stop what he

144

was doing. I saw his silhouette as it passed in front of the window. Then the porch light came on and Warren Miller opened the door just as my father had gotten almost even with it. Warren stepped out onto the lighted porch – I saw his limp. He and my father were standing there together, my father holding the glass gallon jug of gasoline, and Warren holding nothing. It was a strange thing to see. And I thought for an instant that things would be all right, that Warren Miller would take hold of matters, which I knew he could do, and that my father would abandon whatever his plans were – to burn down Warren Miller's house or to throw his own life and mine and my mother's away as if they didn't matter and could just as easily be given up.

'What's going on out here, Jerry?' Warren Miller said, not very loudly. He took a step closer to my father as if he wanted to see better what was happening. And he must've smelled gasoline, because he took a step back. Gasoline must've been everywhere.

My father stood up straight and said something I could not exactly hear, although it sounded like he said 'hat on, hat on,' the same words twice. Then my father squatted down very quickly, exactly in front of Warren Miller, just as if he was about to tie his boot lace. But what he did was strike a match. And I heard Warren say, 'What in the world, Jerry!'

And then the porch was on fire all around them. The bottle my father was holding was on fire inside and out; the boards where my father and Warren were standing were all on fire. A strip of blue and yellow flame moved in an almost lazy way back to the front wall of the house and then down along the porch to the end, and began to go up the wood siding where my father had first splashed gasoline. The house looked all on fire to me then, or at least the front of it did. I began to move myself out of the car in a hurry, because my father's boots and the bottoms of his pants were on fire, and he was trying to hit it all out with his hands, and seemed frantic and was jumping.

Warren Miller simply disappeared. I didn't see him go, but he was gone the instant the flames started. I guessed he was calling for someone to come and help. And my father was left on the front porch alone, trying to keep himself from burning up in the fire he himself had started by some act of jealousy or anger or just insanity—all of which seemed suddenly far in the past and out of any proportion to what was going on.

'I'm on fire here, Joe,' my father called out from the porch as I ran up the concrete steps toward him.

'I know it,' I said.

'I'm sorry,' he said, 'I didn't mean to do this. I certainly didn't.' He seemed both excited and calm at once, even though one of his boots was on fire. He had put out the other boot and the bottom of his pants leg with his hands. And he had moved from the place where he'd set fire to the edge of the porch, so that he was sitting with one leg over the side and the other one, the one with the boot on fire, beside him, and he was hitting it with his bare hand, not very hard but trying to put out the flame. Behind him, the porch was on fire. I could smell it burning and smoking. I could see the wood front of the house in flames, and feel the heat from it on the air.

I took off my jacket when I got to my father, and I put it over his boot foot where it was burning, and I held it down hard and put my arms around it to close out the flames.

'I can't really see myself now,' my father said. 'That's good.' He did not seem excited anymore. His face was very pale, and both his hands looked black as though they'd been burned. He placed them in his lap, and I thought that maybe he didn't know what he had just done, or that he had burned himself and could not feel it. 'Your mother's not in there,' he said to me very calmly. 'Don't worry. I established that.' Light snow was beginning to collect on both of us.

'Why did you light this?' I said, holding on to his foot.

'To get things back on track, I guess,' he said, looking down at his hands in his lap. He raised them a little for some reason, then put them back down. Far away I heard a siren begin. Someone had called the fire department about this. 'My hands don't hurt,' my father said.

'Good,' I said. And I let go of his foot and pulled my jacket from on top of it. It looked fine. It did not look like it had been burning even though I could smell the leather and the gasoline that had soaked it. 'Do you want to get in the car,' I asked, because that is what I wanted.

'No,' he said, 'That's not the right thing to do now.' He turned and looked at the house behind him. There were still flames on the porch and up the boards of the front wall. The bottle he'd had with him had broken. But the fire was dying off from the damp wood and was smoking more than burning, and it did not look to me like the house would burn much more, and would not burn down as I had thought at first. 'This is all unnecessary,' my father said, when he turned around to me. 'Uncalled for. Your mother doesn't trust me. That's all. This whole thing is a matter of trust.' He shook his head and wiggled all ten fingers in his lap as though he was trying to feel them but couldn't, and it made him nervous, and he wanted to do something to feel them again. They were related in his mind to something important.

Warren Miller came out of the front door of his house in a hurry then. He had put on the coat that went with his suit pants, and he had a woman with him, a tall, slender woman with a long, pale face, who had on a man's wool overcoat and silver high-heeled shoes. I recognized the shoes as the ones in Warren's closet. He was moving her in a hurry, with his big limp, down the wooden front steps past where my father and I were, and out onto the driveway away from the house, which he probably thought was burning down but wasn't. He had his hand in the middle of her back. When he got her out to the sidewalk at the end of the driveway, he turned and he looked at us and at the house which still had some blue flames flickering and smoking on the outside walls, but which was mostly not on fire anymore. People up and down the street had come out of their houses and into their yards, including the two older people from next door, who I recognized and who went across the street to watch from the yard there. I could hear someone, a woman's voice, yelling, 'Come see this. You won't believe it. Oh, my Lord.' I began to hear sirens closer and the engines of the pumper truck as it came across the bridge with a bell ringing. And I stood there beside my father, waiting to see what would happen.

'This will turn out better than it seems,' my father said. He was looking around. He must've been amazed at what he'd done, at all the people who were looking at him and at me.

'It'll be all right,' I said. 'Not that much happened.'

'I wish it was all right now,' he said. 'I wish.'

Warren said something to the tall woman in the man's coat. I thought it was his coat, though it was not the one my mother had worn. The woman said something to him and looked at my father and me and shook her head. Then Warren Miller began limping toward us, up onto the grass of his own yard in the melting snow. We were just waiting for him, I guess, and for something to happen to us – for the police or the fire department to come, or whatever would happen officially. My father had decided to stay where he was and to take what was coming to him. He had no place to go. This must've seemed as good as any other place.

'You're a goddamned drunk, aren't you?' Warren Miller said, before he even got to us, while he was still limping across his yard. He was mad. I saw that. His voice seemed deeper than it had when I was in his house the night before. His face was pale and damp. 'God *damn* it, Jerry,' he said. 'You're all drunked up, and you've ruined my house.'

My father didn't say anything to answer. I don't know what he could've said. But when Warren Miller got to where we were—my father sitting on the edge of the porch and me beside him—he grabbed my father by his shirt front, just grabbed up the front of it, and hit him in the face with his fist, hit him so hard my father rocked backward. Though he didn't go far back because Warren kept hold of him. Warren pulled his fist back to hit my father in the face again, but I reached up and put my hands over my father's face, and said very loudly, 'Don't do that. Don't do it again.'

And Warren Miller turned loose of his shirt instantly and put both his hands into his coat pockets. Though he didn't leave, he stayed where he was, did not even move back a step. His glasses looked dirty and fogged up, and his face was wet and so was his suit coat. He was breathing hard. I looked out where people were standing in the street. Someone there was pointing at us or at Warren Miller, who had hit my father. I saw a boy running across the yards to get to a place where he could see better. I heard sirens coming, and I could taste smoke.

'God damn it, you have a son here, Jerry,' Warren Miller said. 'I don't know why you'd do a thing like this.' He was staring at my father, who was blinking his eyes. He wasn't bleeding and there were no marks on his face where Warren had hit him, but he must've been dizzy or sick from it. I wanted to tell Warren to leave, that we were finished, but it was his house we were sitting in front of.

'Who's that?' my father said. He was looking at the woman waiting out on the sidewalk in the long coat and the silver shoes.

'What do you mean?' Warren Miller said. He seemed astonished. 'That's none of your business who that is. It's not your wife.' He was still angry, I could feel it just being beside him. 'I've got a pistol inside there, Jerry,' he said. 'I could shoot you and nobody'd say anything. They'd probably be glad.'

'I know that,' my father said, though I was shocked to hear that.

'How old are you, for God's sake?' Warren Miller said.

'Thirty-nine,' my father said.

'Weren't you a college man? Didn't you attend a college?' Warren Miller said.

'Yes,' my father said.

Warren Miller turned and looked out in the front yard then. Some cars had stopped and the fire truck was blowing its horn to clear a way down the street. But the fire had put itself out by then. The snow had done it, and there wasn't any need to have firemen come.

Warren Miller looked at me, his hands still in his pockets. His blue eyes were wide behind his glasses. 'I knew you were in the house today,' he said. 'I could've broken in there, but I didn't want this to get out of hand.' He shook his head. 'I ought to beat the hell out of you right now.' Then he looked at my father again. I think he was trying to decide what to do, and didn't exactly know what the right thing was. It was a peculiar moment for all of us. 'You should've known about this, Jerry,' Warren Miller said. 'God damn you. You can't stop these things. You can't go off from home and expect people to just stay put. You can't blame anybody but yourself. You're a fool is what you are. And that's all you are.'

'Maybe so,' my father said. 'I'm sorry.' He was staring down. Out in the town I could hear other sirens, ones that had nothing to do with us, but with other people in town who were afraid of fires starting.

'She was throwing things up to see where they'd land,' Warren Miller said. 'It was over before you even knew about it. At least as far as I was concerned.' He turned and looked at the street again.

Headlights from the fire trucks lit the pavement. I could hear the big engines throbbing. In the yard across the street a man was using a hose to wet his roof. Two firemen were walking out of the dark, wearing their big firemen's hats and coats and boots and holding fire extinguisher cans and flashlights. The flames were all out on the house, now. Some neighbors were talking to the firemen who were on the truck. Someone laughed out loud.

'What did you think?' Warren Miller said to my father, who was sitting with his burned hands in his lap, his face beginning to swell from where he'd been punched. 'Don't you think this is a pretty big mistake? What do you think all these people think of you? A house-burner like this. In front of his own son. I'd be ashamed.'

'Maybe they think it was important to me,' my father said. He wiped his hands over his damp face then, and took a deep breath and let it out slowly. I could hear it go out.

'They think *nothing's* important to you,' Warren said loudly. 'They think you wanted to commit suicide, that's all. They feel sorry for you. You're out of your mind.'

He turned around and limped out into the front yard where snow was beginning to frost up on the damp grass, and the firemen were halfway up toward the house, pointing their flashlights in front of them and smiling and beginning to talk. They seemed to know Warren Miller. Warren Miller knew people. And we, my father and I, and my mother, didn't know anyone. We were alone there in Great Falls. Strangers. We only had ourselves to answer for us if things went bad and turned against us as they had done at that moment.

In the end, not very much happened – not what you would expect to happen when one man sets another man's house on fire and gets caught doing it in front of a street filled with people and at a time when they are afraid of fires. People have been hanged for such a thing as that in Montana.

The two firemen who Warren Miller knew came up and

looked at where the fire had burned the porch and around the side of the house. They did not put water on anything, and they didn't talk to my father or me, though Warren told them that there had been a misunderstanding between himself and my father. Both firemen looked at us then, but just briefly. And then Warren Miller went back down to the street and sat in the back of the chief's red car. They talked there while we waited. I saw that Warren signed something. The neighbors began to drift away back inside, and the man who had been hosing his house quit and disappeared. The fire trucks left, and the tall woman who had come out of the house with Warren got cold and went and sat in the Oldsmobile and started it to get the heater going. We were the only ones left outside, still sitting on the lighted porch in the cold snowy night. I could smell the smell of burned wood.

My father did not say anything while we waited. He watched the chief's car, which is what I did, too. Though after a while, maybe fifteen minutes, Warren Miller climbed out of the chief's car, walked down the sidewalk in front of his own house and up the driveway, where he got in his car, the one he'd been in with my mother and where the woman was waiting on him, and they backed out and drove away down Prospect Street into the night. I didn't know where they were going, though I never saw him again in my life.

It was then that my father said, very calmly, 'They're probably going to arrest me. A fireman can arrest you, too. They're qualified. I'm sorry about all of this.'

One of the two firemen got out of the chief's car then. He was the older of the two who had come up and looked at the house. He was smoking a cigarette and he threw it in the grass as he walked up on the yard to where we were still sitting on the edge of the porch. We both knew not to leave, though no one had said that.

'This is a misunderstanding up here, is what I've been

told,' the fireman said to my father when he was close enough. He looked at my father once and then looked past him at the damaged house where the fronts of most of the boards had been burned black. He did not look at me. He was a tall man, in his sixties. He had on a heavy black asbestos coat and rubber boots, and no hat on. I had seen him before, but I did not remember where.

'I guess it could've been,' my father said, calmly.

'It's your lucky day today,' the fireman said. He looked at my father again quickly. He was just standing there in front of us, talking. 'This man who lives here stood up for you. I wouldn't have myself. I know what you did, and I know what it's about.'

'Okay,' my father said. The fireman looked away again. I knew he hated the thought of both of us, and that it embarrassed him and embarrassed my father, too.

'You ought to get killed for doing a thing like this,' the fireman said. 'I'd kill you if I caught you.'

'You don't need to say that. It's right,' my father said.

'Your son's seen plenty now.' The fireman looked at me for the first time. He stepped toward me and put his big hand on my shoulder. 'He won't forget *you*,' he said to my father, then he squeezed my shoulder very hard.

'No, he won't,' my father said.

The fireman suddenly laughed out loud, 'Hah,' and shook his head. It was a strange thing to do. I almost felt myself smile, though I didn't want to. And I didn't. 'You can't choose who your old man is,' he said to me. He was smiling, his hand still on my shoulder, as if we knew a joke together. 'Mine was a son-of-a-bitch. A soapstone son-of-a-bitch.'

'That's too bad,' my father said.

'Come down to the fire station next week, son,' the fireman said to me. 'I'll show you how things work.' He looked at my father again. 'Your wife's probably worried about you, bud,' he said. 'Take your son home where he belongs.'

'All right,' my father said. 'That's a good idea.'

'Your old man ought to be in jail, son,' the fireman said, 'but he's not.' Then he walked away, back across the yard and down the street to where his red car was and where the younger fireman sat in the driver's seat waiting. They turned around in the street—just for that moment turning their flashing light on, then switching it off—and drove away.

Across the street a woman stood at her front door watching the two of us—my father and me. She said something to someone who was behind her, someone out of sight inside the house. I could only see her head turn and her lips move, but I couldn't hear any words.

'People think they live in eternity, don't they?' my father said. Something about the woman across the street made him say that. I don't know what it was. 'Everything just goes on forever. Nothing's final.' He stood up then. And he seemed stiff, as though he'd been hurt, though he hadn't been. He stood up straighter, looking out over the houses across the street toward town. A light went off in the house across the street. 'Wouldn't that be gratifying,' he said.

'I guess so,' I said. And I stood up, too.

'This won't stay important forever, Joe,' my father said. 'You'll forget most of it. I won't, but you will. I wouldn't even blame you if you hated me, right now.'

'I don't,' I said. And I didn't hate him. Not at all. I could not see him very clearly then, but he was my father. Nothing had changed as far as that was concerned. I loved him in spite of it all.

'You can get carried away with how things were once, and not how you need to make them better,' my father said. 'Don't do that.' He began to walk in a stiff gait to our car. It was parked where it had been the whole time, on the street in front of Warren Miller's house. 'That's my one piece of good advice to you,' he said. I heard him take a deep breath and let it out. Far off on another street I heard a siren begin again, and I thought there must be another fire going. And I started after my father, across the yard where it was not snowing anymore. I knew he was not even thinking about me at that moment, but about some other problem I did not figure in. Though I wondered where we would go next, and where I would spend the night, and what would happen to me tomorrow and the day after that. I must've believed that I lived in eternity myself then, that I had no final answers and none were being asked of me. And, in fact, even while I walked away from Warren Miller's house that night in the cold October air, everything that had just happened was beginning already to fade from my thinking, just as my father said it would. I felt calm and I began to believe that things would not turn out so badly after all. At least I thought they probably would not turn out that way for me.

THERE ARE SEVERAL LETTERS my mother wrote me in the time after that—1960 and '61. In one she said, 'Try not to think of your life as being different from other boys' lives, Joe. That would be a help.' In another she said, 'You may think that I am the unconventional one in this, but your father is very unconventional. I am not very much.' And in another she said, 'I am wondering if my own parents ever saw the world as I do now. We are always looking for absolutes and not finding them. You get an itch for the real thing, and you are not one yourself. Love, at least, seems very permanent to me.'

This was at a time, I believe, when she was living in Portland, Oregon, and was hoping to find a job. Her letters had 'The Davenport Hotel' letterhead on them, although for some reason I did not think she was staying there. I did not know very much about her at all during that time and actually thought of her as lost to us, forever.

It is possible, and I have thought this over the years since then, that my father must've felt that all forward motion in his life had come to a stop that night at Warren Miller's house, and that Warren was right—that my father wished Warren would come out and shoot him right there. And that was why he didn't run away. When things in your life turn against you and do it all at once, as it happened to my father, there must be a strong desire to end it for yourself, to give life back and let other, stronger people—people like Warren Miller—carry it on to wherever it will go. Or at least there is a desire to become a smaller part of something larger in life, something that will take charge of you as though you were a child. My mother may have felt the same way about things.

I wondered, in the days that followed, when my mother was moving to the Helen Apartments and then out of there in a hurry, and out of town, if I would ever see the world as *I* had seen it before then, when I did not even know I saw it. Or if you just got used to parting with things, and because you were young you parted with them faster; or if in fact none of that thinking was important at all, and things stayed mostly the same in spite of small changes, so that when you faced the worst and went past it what you found there was nothing. Nothing has its own badness, but it does not last forever. And what there is to learn from almost any human experience is that your own interests do not usually come first where other people are concerned—even the people who love you—and that is all right. It can be lived with.

The fire my father had left home to fight did not die out easily, but lasted a long time—not the way anyone would think, that a fire is just a thing that can be put out. It did not threaten towns, but it smoldered all winter, and then in the spring it blew up again in a smaller way and smoke we could feel in our eyes was in the air, though my father did not go out to fight it.

In the spring when I was back in school, I tried to throw the javelin, but I was no good at it and did not throw it far. Not far enough. So I quit. My father said that he and I would start to golf again when the weather improved, and in time we did, and in general I felt that my life *was* like other boys' lives. I did not have friends. I had met a girl I liked but I did not know what to do where she was concerned, did not know a place to go with her, and didn't have a car to take her anywhere. In truth, I did not have a life except for the life at home with my father. But that did not seem unusual to me then, or even now.

In early March, Warren Miller died. I read about it in the newspaper. The story said a 'lengthy illness' was the cause and did not go on further, except that he died at home. I realized he must've thought he was sick and dying when he knew my mother. And I wondered if she had known that, or if she had ever seen him again after that night in our house. I decided that she had – maybe in Portland, where she was, or some other town. I tried to imagine what they talked about and decided it was only what all of us already knew. I think she loved him. She certainly said she did, and I think she loved my father too. There is an old saying that when you have two you really have none. And that is what I finally thought about my mother, wherever she was, in whatever city, doing whatever she was doing alone. She had none, and I was sorry for her for that to be so.

My father did not seem unhappy to me. I do not think he heard from my mother, even though I received letters at home. I think he believed she was not making a new start in life but was continuing something onward, and that he should do the same thing. He found a job selling insurance for a while in the winter, and when that did not go well enough he took a job at a sporting goods store in the middle of town and sold golf clubs and tennis rackets and baseball mitts. For a time in the spring he had two wire cages behind our house, cages he'd built himself, and kept a rabbit and a pheasant and a small speckled partridge he actually found in the street. And life went on for us on a different scale from how it had gone on. On a smaller human scale. There is no doubting that. But it went on. We survived it.

And then at the end of March, in 1961, just as it was beginning to be spring, my mother came back from wherever she had been. In a while she and my father found a way to settle the difficulties that had been between them. And though they may both have felt that something had died between them, something they may not even have been aware of until it was gone and disappeared from their lives forever, they must've felt—both of them—that there was something of themselves, something important, that could not live at all in any other way but by their being together, much as they had been before. I do not know exactly what that something was. But that is how our life resumed after then, for the little time that I was at home. And for many years after that. They lived together—that was their life—and alone. Though God knows there is still much to it that I myself, their only son, cannot fully claim to understand.

A Note on the Author

Richard Ford was born in Jackson, Mississippi, in 1944. He has published six novels and three collections of stories, including *The Sportswriter*, *Independence Day*, *Wildlife*, *A Multitude of Sins* and most recently *The Lay of the Land*. *Independence Day* was awarded the Pulitzer Prize and the PEN/Faulkner Award for Fiction.

A MULTITUDE OF SINS

**'Ford's sheer mastery of the short-story form
is jaw-dropping'**
Guardian

'Ten sexy, grown-up stories about marriage and
adultery, passion and infidelity, disappointment and
revenge. Ford is a smooth master of his art'
Financial Times

With perhaps his fiercest intensity to date, Richard
Ford, America's most unflinching chronicler of
modern life, is drawn to amorous relationships inside,
out and to the sides of marriage. In these extraordinary stories all human relations, our entire sense of
right and wrong, are put into vivid and unforgettable
play.

'Ford's is the voice of twentieth-century America;
funny, human, sad and real'
Eileen Battersby, *Irish Times*

'Now in its full maturity, his writing rolls and twists
with complexities and sadness and humour; his char-
acters may not often have lives they call their own,
but his sentences always do'
Observer

Buy this book at www.bloomsbury.com/richardford

ROCK SPRINGS

'A collection of stunning impact, which marks
Ford's arrival at the pinnacle of his craft'
Sunday Times

'These are beautifully imagined and crafted stories.
By turns heart rending and wickedly funny – and just
plain wicked. Richard Ford is a born storyteller with
an inimitable lyric voice – and *Rock Springs* is the
poetry of realism'
Joyce Carol Oates

The stories in this celebrated collection are about ordinary women and children. Unemployed, on the way
back to prison, marriages in tatters, they confront their
fates with hard-won optimism and flashes of insight.

'The people in this marvellous book of short stories
have no fixed points; they have moved away from
their childhood town, or their first marriage, and lost
track of parents who have usually split up themselves.
They live on the fringes of legality, matter of fact
about car theft and bad cheques. Motels and inter-
state highways are the natural landscape of their lives
... *Rock Springs* confirms Ford's place among our
finest writers'
The Times

Buy this book at www.bloomsbury.com/richardford

A PIECE OF MY HEART

'This is quality writing in the highest American
tradition of Faulkner, Hemingway and Steinbeck'
The Times

'Superb ... Brutally real and at the same time haunting
... One of those rare surprises that come along every
few years'
Jim Harrison

Robard Hughes has raced across the country in pursuit
of a woman, and Sam Newell is hunting for the
missing part of himself. On an uncharted island on the
Mississippi, both these godless pilgrims find what they
have been searching for in an explosion of shocking
violence. The novel that launched the career of one of
America's late-twentieth-century masters, *A Piece of
My Heart* is a *tour de force* that does justice to Ford's
diverse literary gifts: his unerring eye for detail, his
pitch-perfect ear for dialogue, and his sharp understanding of human nature.

'I am enormously delighted to make the acquaintance
of this muscular American writer, whose glowering
prose, in hot mode or in cool, throbs with the weight
of the vast continent he lovingly embraces'
Independent

Buy this book at www.bloomsbury.com/richardford

THE SPORTSWRITER

'Ford is a masterful writer'
Raymond Carver

'A devastating chronicle of contemporary alienation'
New York Times

'Richard Ford's sportswriter is a rare bird in life and
nearly extinct in fiction'
Tobias Wolff

At dawn on Good Friday every year, Frank Bascombe
and his wife meet to pay their respects at the grave of
their firstborn. This year Frank plans to spend the
Easter weekend with a new girlfriend while on assign-
ment for his magazine. What might have been an
idyllic adventure becomes a succession of calamities
that extinguish almost all the carefully nourished
equilibrium of a man grappling with the failure of love
and the death of his son.

The end and the aftermath of a marriage, the
emotional dislocation and the discovery of a new life
while in the embrace of troubled memories of the old
have seldom been more harrowingly plotted. *The
Sportswriter* is also a wistful, very funny and always
human illumination of domestic and sexual anguish
through the story of Frank Bascombe, its hero, the
sportswriter.

Buy this book at www.bloomsbury.com/richardford

INDEPENDENCE DAY

**Winner of the Pulitzer Prize and the
PEN/Faulkner Award**

'The best novel out of America in many years ...
simply a masterpiece'
John Banville, *Guardian*

'It is nothing less than the story of the 20th century
itself ... Eloquently, with awkward grace, in his
novels about an ordinary man, Ford has created
an extraordinary epic'
The Times

After the disintegration of his family, the ruin of his
career and an affair with a much younger woman,
Frank Bascombe decides that the surest route to a
'normal' American life is to become an estate agent in
Haddam, New Jersey. Frank blunders through the
suburban citadels of the Eastern Seaboard and avoids
engaging in life until the sudden, cataclysmic events of
a Fourth-of-July weekend with his son jolt him back.

The sequel to *The Sportswriter* and the first novel to
win the Pulitzer Prize and the PEN/Faulkner Award
in the same year, *Independence Day* is a landmark in
American Literature.

THE ULTIMATE
GOOD LUCK

'His prose has a taut, cinematic quality that bathes his story with the same hot, mercilessly white light that scorches Mexico'
New York Times

'Ford's taut, compelling prose is as piercingly clear as a police siren. No other storyteller writes about the alienated and uncommitted with such mastery'
Sunday Times

Harry Quinn and his girlfriend Rae head to Oaxaca, Mexico, to spring Rae's brother Sunny from jail and protect him from the sinister drug dealer he is suspected of having double-crossed. But instead of a simple jailbreak, Harry and Rae fall into a nightmarish series of entanglements with expat whores and Zapotec Indians. The Cocaine Era's answer to Graham Greene, this exquisitely choreographed novel tracks Rae's and Harry's inexorable descent into the Mexican underworld, where only a stroke of ultimate good luck can keep them alive.

'So hard-boiled and tough that it might have been written on the back of a trench coat. A grand *Maltese Falcon* of a novel'
Stanley Elkin

WOMEN WITH MEN

'Richard Ford is one of the best writers in
America. Potentially the very best'
Gordon Burn

'At once funny and heartbreaking, as Ford's work
usually is ... This is fiction at its finest'
John Banville

'Here are three perfect "long" stories, so sinuously
entwined and so subtly echoing one another that the
whole towers like a great novel'
Mail on Sunday

Three outstanding novellas, depicting with a heart-
wrenching honesty the limits of human love. Against
settings that range from the alleyways of Paris to the
northern plains of Montana and the suburbs of
Chicago, Richard Ford dramatises the impasses and
abysses that exist in all romantic relationships.
Capturing men and women at defining moments of
truth – whether during seismic arguments, or simply
in the course of everyday life – Ford affirms yet again
his reputation as one of the great American writers of
our time.

'This sparkling collection sees the author of
Independence Day at the top of his form. The stories
are both powerful fictions in their own right and a
perfectly formed triptych'
Sunday Telegraph

Buy this book at www.bloomsbury.com/richardford

THE LAY OF THE LAND

'Bascombe's voice remains one of the most generous
and wise in contemporary fiction, the honest
testimony of a pilgrim seeking the transcendent
in a decidedly mundane world'
Stephen Amidon, *Sunday Times*

With *The Sportswriter*, in 1985, Richard Ford began a
cycle of novels that ten years later – after *Independence
Day* won both the Pulitzer Prize and the PEN/
Faulkner Award – was hailed by *The Times* as 'an
extraordinary epic [that] is nothing less than the story
of the 20th century itself'.

Frank Bascombe's story resumes in the fall of 2000,
with the presidential election still hanging in the
balance and Thanksgiving looming before him with
all the perils of a post-nuclear family get-together.
He's now, at fifty-five, plying his trade as a real estate
agent on the Jersey shore and contending with health,
marital, and familial issues that have his full attention.
This is Richard Ford's first novel in more than a
decade: the funniest, most engaging and explosive
book he's written.

Buy this book at www.bloomsbury.com/richardford